Gray

JAMES FOUCHE

For Madeleine,

The world is a bit darker without you here,
but your light still moves us
— even from afar.

gray (Gy): A unit of absorbed radiation equal to the dose of one joule of energy absorbed per kilogram of matter, or 100 rad. The unit is named for the British physician L. Harold Gray (1905-1965), an authority on the use of radiation in the treatment of cancer.

- Glossary of radiation units at www.radiologyinfo.com

CHAPTER 1

I was about to pass out when the car finally drew to a halt. The hum of the motor died down. There came a click of a locking mechanism letting go, then a wave of light spilled over me as the car's boot groaned open. The morning sun crawled deeper into the boot space and wrapped around my body, drawing the ache out of my joints and the cold out of my muscles.

The grey bag covering my head added to the claustrophobia. Though porous enough, it revealed very little. The only clear movement I saw was through a narrow slit when I looked down. The bag had the characteristics of a large woollen sock. It certainly smelled like one.

Car doors slammed shut and muted voices soon became a stream of street lingo bragging about illicit events. Through the wool, I made out two shadowy figures against the blue skyline.

Seconds later, two sets of hands tugged at my clothes and limbs until I stood upright on what must have been a tarred road surface. My hands were cable-tied behind my back. I swung my head this way and that to find some discernment on the other end of my head sock, but it was disorientating.

1

I heard dogs barking, sprinklers *tsik-tsik-tsik-trrrring*, and a lonely cicada calling for company. I could no longer smell the sea floating on the air. There was no salt, only construction dust and dried grass. My senses, however, were not as sharp as they had been a couple of months ago.

I surmised that we had come up to the Northern Suburbs of Cape Town. The boot trip had lasted about two hours, which would have been enough to cover that distance while adhering to the speed limits. I was thumb-sucking the duration, but it sounded fair. Besides, I couldn't check my wristwatch with my hands bound. Nor could I scratch the itch below my knee.

I was nudged forward. My heart was eager to follow my captors, but my feet were reluctant, like two blocks of cement dragging along a shallow riverbed. Looking down, I saw the tips of my old blue sneakers. I curled up my toes but saw no movement at the tip. Besides the itch, my legs were numb from the waist down. I willed my feet to cooperate. A long journey lay ahead.

Over a small curb, up a series of steps, over a carpeted section and onto a black plastic sheet, my feet went, one in front of the other, like hooves clopping into an abattoir. A white chair entered my narrow strip of vision. The firm hand resting on my shoulder applied pressure, urging me to sit.

I was worn out from wrestling with the cable ties and not having any water. Rolling over every time the driver took a left had sent me smacking into the edge of the boot's metal framework, then back again until a tire iron wedged into my back. In contrast, the chair looked inviting to me. I welcomed the opportunity to rest.

Once seated, the grey head sock was plucked from my head

as though a magician was unveiling a bunny to an audience. A blast of blinding light filled my periphery. I winced, blinked, and allowed my eyes to adjust. My surroundings bled through my blindness and took shape in front of me, outer edges first, then the inner bits followed.

The room was completely empty; void of furniture or character that would indicate what type of room it was. White camping chairs were placed in no discernible order across the cemented floor, though I noticed mine centred in the builder's plastic sheet. In one corner was a small wooden ladder and two large buckets of paint, on which were piled trays, rollers, brushes and a cartridge of elastic sealant.

Opposite me was the outline of a large wooden chair. The figure seated in the chair was veiled in shards of shadow. Though obscured by the light that pierced through the large windows, the calm, crisp voice told me who I was in company with.

"So, let's have it then," he said in a steady monotone that belied his true intentions.

I knew this man. I knew his intentions. I have studied him for weeks on end. That gave me a slight advantage – because he didn't know me at all. All he knew about me was what I wanted him to know, and that was very little. Then again, I couldn't say with certainty what exactly he had been told about me, because I hadn't been present at the time.

Over the last couple of months, I had found that the world was filled with people who needed only a glimpse of an idea to believe it, whether true or not. Manipulating them had been easier than I had imagined. They'd believed every word I had fed them. They had to have believed it or else we wouldn't be here, stuck in this room on a hot afternoon. I also knew we were in this room because his other more secretive locations had been rendered less secretive because of my meddling.

"My hands," I complained. "Can you untie me?"

It's funny how I could sense him smiling at me without seeing a smile on his face. I had complete faith that he would do whatever I asked of him, at least for the next couple of hours. But I had to push the boundaries early on. If I didn't prepare my audience at the start, I'd be dead within the hour.

I had no doubt that they wanted to kill me at that moment. Soon they would have ample reason to act on that desire. I was about to tear their worlds apart. Similarly, I had just cause to make their lives hell. And I would do so at my own peril. I was prepared for any outcome.

His eyes beamed at me for so long that I became uncomfortable. He shrugged and nodded at someone behind me. I couldn't see the guy approaching, but by the slow, heavy sounds of his boots it sounded like a big man. I heard the flicking sound of a pocketknife, felt the cold blade slide into the tiny gap where my wrists joined and the cable ties snapping apart.

Freedom, sort of. I brought my hands around, first scratching the spot below my knee, then studied the purple rings around my wrists and massaged the bruises. My fingers had a bluish tinge to them. The cable ties had started cutting into my wrists, pressing through the soft skin at the joints. I remembered a time when my skin hadn't been this fine. It was only recently that my vitality had departed from me.

"I need some water," I said to the man behind me, then to my captor, "Please."

Without shifting his gaze, he flicked a finger. Someone left the room in search of water.

There were scuffling sounds in one dark corner, followed by a soft groan. I had heard that display of annoyance before. I knew him well, too. Both these men, night and day to the common eye, had been dealt the same burden of being under my close observation. Burden because I had intended to be a burden to the utmost degree. Revenge could make one throw caution to the wind. Oh, bittersweet revenge. It was like a bad investment: no matter how much money you pumped into it, it could never bring you joy.

The man hiding in the corner stepped into view. His name was Shane Collins. He was short and muscular, with thin lips that betrayed a sly smile. He was naturally short-tempered, and when he snapped, violence followed. Even now, I saw the effort it required of him not to attack me with his bare hands.

The man seated in the wooden chair was Denvor Daniels. Tall and well-groomed, he looked like a salesman. He was twice as dangerous as Shane because he was methodical, and sociopathic, contrasting Shane's predictability. Denvor applied patience to his retaliatory advances. Fortunately, he was not as reckless as Shane and refrained from making waves. Shane enjoyed headlines while Denvor hid in the shadows. He was a puppet master, which had benefitted the pair when they had been in partnership years before.

Since then, both have become career criminals. While they had made peace with their illicit affairs, they had become mortal enemies. Biological opposites, twins by trade, and permanently at war, like two worms fighting inside the same rotten apple. They were bitter to the bone and fiercely territorial, but the forgotten friendship often stayed their fury.

They had no idea who I was. Where did I come from? Who

did I work for? How did I manage to gather so much money in their territory without them knowing about it? *And where was the money stashed now?* Those were the questions they had been fed.

"So, where is it?" Shane said, tapping his foot loudly.

Not the opening question I had been expecting, though I realized that Shane was all about the bottom line.

I coughed, hinting that I couldn't possibly carry on without a sip of water.

The bottle of water previously called for appeared on the small table in front of me, beads of condensation already forming on the outside. I wondered whether someone down the ranks had run to the corner shop.

"Could I have sparkling?" I ventured, gauging how far I could push. Their combined reactions informed me that it was too soon. "This will do," I said, sucking greedily at what could be the last water I'd ever drink. I finished half the bottle, drinking until tears welled up, then screwed the cap back on and leaned back.

Shane opened his hands in anticipation, mouth agape. He leaned forward until he was hovering over the table, then hissed, "Where's the money? And who are you working for?"

Still massaging my wrists, I scanned the room again. It was a sad display of feigned machismo, a poster ad for toxic masculinity. Twelve men scattered about, like fishermen without a vessel. The nature of the business they were in suggested they were all armed with some type of weapon. I remembered all these men. I had studied them, too. I could have murdered every one of them. I could have killed them in their most private places, in front of their loved ones, while they were taking a piss. I had planned to pick them all off slowly, one by one, in gruesome ways, but unintended contemplation had steered me elsewhere.

Time was a precious commodity and pernicious when in abundance, but when time became instantly reduced to crumbs, it was made clear to me that time would not, as the famous saying stated, heal all wounds.

"Okay, let me tell you where I got the money, then all this will make more sense."

Both men wanted to separate me from my newly acquired fortune, especially since they believed I was muscling in on their joint territory, and because a series of anonymous tips had caused police teams to raid both their storage facilities. They thought I was the competition because I had paid local hooligans to sow those seeds in their turf. What they were unsure about was whether I was independent or working for the competition in the Southern Suburbs.

I had centre stage. I had this one opportunity to do things my way. *Guide my tongue. Let me say the right thing at the right time.*

CHAPTER 2

My father died when I was still young, leaving my mother behind to take care of me and my brother Allan. He was two years my senior, and two sizes bigger than me. My mother was a simple woman who believed in morals and hard work. She slaved day and night to get us through school. The day I graduated, my joy was overshadowed by a car accident that claimed the lives of both my mother's parents, my only surviving grandparents. Something broke inside of her that day. With no husband or sibling to turn to for comfort and two demanding boys to care for, my mother let herself go. She squeezed the best of herself into preparing us for the world.

After school I sought employment and, sadly, I found it. I began as a casual merchandiser at a big retail company in a mall, while my brother pursued the wonderful underpaid world of education. The retail industry swallowed me in as a youth and spat me out as an overworked manager a couple of years later. I was drained, but eager to fight back. After numerous aptitude tests, I qualified for a position as a junior financial adviser at a large firm in the city. Here I met my wife, Brenda.

Back then she was a secretary at the firm. The first day I arrived at the office Brenda was there to greet the newcomers. Her hair hung level with her shoulders; she had thick and springy, voluptuous curls that drove me wild. On that first day, she led the newbies, a mixed group of about ten or so, to an empty office where she prepped us for the induction process. I was amazed at how efficient and orderly she was. While we watched hours of tutorials, I kept picturing this pretty girl at reception. During our lunch break, they brought in coffee and snacks. I was disheartened to see another woman pushing in the tea trolley. It was a childish disappointment, but I couldn't help it.

My infatuation grew with each passing minute, serving as a distraction during group assignments. After our induction, we lined up at reception to sign out and receive our entry cards. There she was, passing out smiles. My heart skipped when the other woman came around to assist Brenda. She motioned me forward with a wave of the finger and a grumpy expression. I signed the documents, but Brenda kept pulling my eyes to her side of the counter. As she busied herself, I studied her every move. I loved studying people. I still do. This was different, though. She had a mesmerizing quality that drew me in and shut out the world.

Then came our inevitable introduction. Attempting to make eye contact before leaving, I walked into a frameless glass door. I broke my nose and two fingers. The office manager claimed it as a record for their firm, with me having to complete an Injured-on-Duty application the same day I signed my Contract of Employment.

I eventually asked her out to coffee. Then followed it up with supper at a fancy restaurant, fully funded by my first paycheck.

We clicked instantly. Her intricacies and my inadequacies complemented each other. For some reason, we were both careful and reluctant in the love department. We evaluated one another from a safe distance.

One day, she invited me along for a morning hike at the base of Devil's Peak. It was days after the arrival of Spring. The air was crisp. The overbearing smell of fynbos pressed in on us from all sides. After the walk along the footpaths, we sat on the cold granite steps that led up to the monument of the Rhodes Memorial. She removed a thermal flask and two cups, then poured out the coffee she had prepared. We sat in silence and watched the sun claw its way free from a clump of trees in the distance. Her face glowed as the bronze rays spread across her cheeks. I was captivated by her. That was our sixth date. I leaned over the coffee cups and stared into her eyes. Our reluctance wavered and we closed the space between us with a kiss.

I returned from that morning hike a married man. At least, in my mind I did. I remembered sending Allan a text, saying that I had met my future wife. We had so much in common. We preferred the woods over the sea, loved to hike together, made a mean paintball team, and we killed at 30 Seconds and Charades. She danced and I watched. I cycled and she watched. She was the pink gin to my craft beer.

I proposed a couple of months later and she said yes.

After we were married, we opened our own advisory office. Word of mouth brought in plenty of business. I was honest and hard-working. Middle-class folk could relate to me on that level. It helped that my brother and his wife, Satí, brought in more business from colleagues at their respective jobs. It turned out teachers were getting poor advice on their retirement planning, so I restructured their savings to work in their favour. I was a master at estate planning, especially at restructuring wills to expedite the winding up of estates after the testator had passed on. My motivation was the memory of how my mother had struggled after my father's passing.

Brenda was my helper in more ways than one. As the years went by, she became so much a part of me that we became one entity. Our relationship thrived on a mutual display of simpatico. We bought a little house not far from the business, yet far enough to be out of the humdrum of city life. We prepared ourselves for the dozens of children we were planning to have.

Although, the children never came. Due to an inexplicable display of biological indolence from both parties, we were unable to become pregnant. Parenthood eluded the ideal parents. The irony of it didn't escape me. The sum of our attempts to conceive had made our dream nightmarish by comparison. If children were the fruits of life, then the inability to have children was the rot of life. There was something to be said here about the sadness and disdain spawned by the barren womb. I have yet to find anything more distressing and drawn out in its haunting. Be it a curse or a result of cruel biological mathematics, I cannot say, but the realization that the soil would remain fruitless no matter how powerful the seed was as crippling a blow as there ever could be. And to further be informed that the seed was substandard was even more crippling. It could drive anyone to tears and prayers, the only resolve that had merit in today's world. Subconsciously, we siloed ourselves from friends with children and drew closer into each other. We contemplated adoption, but in our hope-fueled delays, this goalpost kept being pushed back until it was abandoned altogether.

In keeping with the woe that followed me around, our business collapsed without warning. This was in large part due to industry adjustments and regulations, as well as increasing business costs. I was forced to find placement at a small insurance firm, but a recessionary dip and a subsequent financial crunch caused people to cancel existing policies, which dried up my recurring commission.

I nearly drowned. Financial stress has a way of bringing about sleepless nights, of which there were many. So it was that I found myself down again, and so it was that the other part of me took it upon herself to find a job as a legal secretary to support the house.

Little did I know that our lack of finances would soon be flung into an unquenchable excess of funds through no effort of my own. One might wonder about the inconceivable journey from pauper to millionaire. Regardless of how rare and exceptional this transformational cocoon phase proved to be, I was evidence that it could occur at any moment. However, this transition was a somewhat vexing experience, and the consequence of obtaining abundant wealth was one I would not wish upon another living soul.

A familiar proverb suggests that a fool and his fortune soon part ways. That always made me think of a case study about lotto winners, which we worked on during my induction week. Statistically, lotto winners were the most at risk of burning through their earnings or dying before they could enjoy it. As a financial adviser, I saw my fair share of squandered inheritance, blasted on earthly pleasures, assuring beneficiaries and heirs of mere months of joy, followed by years of rehabilitation to remedy their addiction to spending. Money came and went. Good fortune was given and soon taken away.

Thus my consternation that, by some great existential riddle of Jobian equivalence, circumstances sought me out to inflate my bank balance. And how fitting that the onset of my wealth would be kicked into motion by a series of tragedies.

It was about a year before my abduction. My wife was away on a business trip for the better part of a week. She seldom went away, and when she did, I quickly grew tired of the quiet house. The empty bed, the depressing echo of my shoes bouncing back at me when I swept through the kitchen, and our cat Moscow's sad meow when I forgot to feed it. It was amazing how she filled the home with warmth, but when she left, the house was unnerved, and it drew all life back into the plasterwork. The first night, I loved having the bed to myself, to do my human starfish impersonation, but then the bed grew cold and, when the lights went out, I only had the weight of the ceiling to force me to sleep.

With no childless friends to socialize with and my mother living in another city, I found myself watching the second hand twitch its way across the stolid face of the wall clock. Allan and Satí lived nearby, which made it easy to stay in touch, though we seldom did. He called me up that Friday morning and suggested I join them for supper and a movie. I suspect Brenda might have lobbied a charity call to Satí.

Sharing my fear of unnecessarily dirtying dishes, Allan insisted we go to a restaurant beforehand. While humming and hawing, phone in hand, considering how to decline a sympathy invitation, I glanced at the picture frame on my office desk. It contained a photo of Brenda leaning against the base of a tall Crape Myrtle tree in bloom, taken at a Christmas function the year before. Her sincere eyes and infectious smile leapt out at me from the entanglement of bright pink, cone-shaped clusters that spotted the tree's long limbs. The sight of our empty bed flashed in my mind, the sheets tousled and crinkled on my side, flat and lifeless on Brenda's, Moscow warming the feet of a ghost where my wife usually lay.

I agreed to join them.

Allan was a demanding figure: big head, large round chin, dangling arms, and hands that could crush coconuts. He stooped when he walked as though his shoulders housed an unbearable burden. An inapproachable hulk of grumpiness with a gentle teddy bear hiding inside. His contentment was ambitious, admirable. It was no surprise that Allan found joy in the city's worst classrooms, a place where he could impart his peace and moral fibre to the broken young minds where pain lingered.

Allan was a teacher and Satí a youth counsellor, both government employees. She was the daughter of Samir Parker, a once-poor Indian migrant, and Caroline, an aspiring English missionary. Her parents had travelled the world to establish community outreach projects. When Satí was born, their lives became somewhat subdued. They raised their daughter in poverty, teaching her the value of sharing. When Satí finished school, she was a beautiful dark-haired woman with a horde of eligible suitors at her beck and call. Instead of auctioning off her independence and taking a man, Satí became involved with outreach projects in her neighbourhood, a sure-fire way to alienate herself from the rich young boys whose nightlife consisted of partying and drinking. She did a stint in Africa, where she met Allan, who was teaching kids at a village in Zambia at the time. Their romance was an intoxicating one. When two people share a passion, they become an unstoppable force, and so it was with Allan and Satí.

For the sake of relevance, I must add that a couple of years ago, Samir Parker, having lived a full life, leaned back in his chair one morning and left this world. Some months after Samir's stroke, Caroline suffered the same stroke on the way to a shopping mall. The similarity was eerie, but it was inspiring to hear Satí talk about their sudden deaths so candidly. At her mother's funeral, Satí highlighted that her parents had grown so close that even in death they could not be apart for too long. It was, in fact, her intense bond with Allan that superseded the deaths of her parents. Little did the optimistic Satí know then that her immediate future would be plagued by similar emotional trials.

That night, they picked me up in their red Toyota. With time at our disposal, we went to a small restaurant opposite the mall before heading to the movies. I knew Allan would offer to pay, but I preferred to pay my way even if it killed me. They waited in the car while I ran across the street to an automated teller machine to draw money. I had this habit of stuffing money into someone's pockets or ashtray without them knowing about it. I had an unyielding ethical backbone, and quick fingers to boot.

The machine beeped as the transaction was concluded, then the notes peeled out of the cash dispenser slot. Waiting for the receipt, I heard a loud clapping sound that was unfamiliar to me. Though loud, it was surprisingly muted. It was followed by a smacking sound next to my head. I stared intently at the ATM's glass partitioning, studying the tiny hole that hadn't been there seconds before. The spiderweb of cracks that spiralled outward marred my confused reflection. Then another loud clap rippled through the peaceful night.

My diaphragm flexed into a strained convex dome and my legs gave way to a crouch. My breath took off as my lungs were forced into confinement. Filled with adrenaline, my heartbeat clucked in my ears like the hungry idle of a muscle car. A haunting scream was loosed, drifting in the air until another gunshot rang out, cutting through my stupefaction.

With money clasped in hand, I scampered across the pavement toward the safety of an old VW Beetle. From there I could observe the commotion in the parking lot from a safe distance. It felt like an action movie, only I was the cameraman.

I could see the restaurant to my left, the parking area in front of it and the extended parking section off to the right, with the mall and our awaiting cinema seats in the distance beyond that. It was in the parking area, well-lit by streetlights, where men were crouched behind two cars. Near the narrow stretch in front of the restaurant, another group of men were concealed behind a blue BMW. The two groups discharged their weapons without the slightest concern about where bullets landed, firing rounds haphazardly as if they were shooting with water pistols in a school playground. People were running, dropping to the pavement, covering their heads, sliding over hoods of cars, diving behind shrubs and searching for any object of concealment.

Hiding on the outskirts, I looked on in disbelief as a bullet cracked through the restaurant's front window. A mass of cracks took shape, then the entire window collapsed in a shower of shiny shards. A waitress clasped her bloodied arm and went down screaming. A brave patron tackled another waitress to the ground. They disappeared out of sight at the other end of a salad bar, lettuce and cocktail tomatoes taking flight as they toppled over the display case. A car window burst inward. A tire let out a long sigh from where its rubber body had been pierced.

Another wayward slug smacked into the tar next to my Volkswagen shield. A homeless guy sharing my shelter grabbed my shirt and pulled me back behind the car's wheel, his kindness like an alarm clock inside my mind. At the sound of approaching sirens, the parking area fell silent. A total of nineteen shots had been fired. I remembered that it was an uneven number.

As the two groups made their separate getaways, I ventured a quick peek. I saw two faces that night. One was that of Shane jumping into the back of a blue BMW. The other was that of Denvor walking boldly to his car. Both cars sped off, spewing out gravel and leaving an air of battle smoke in their wake.

The sirens grew louder, then died down as police vans arrived on the scene. The blue flashes of the emergency response lights had a mesmerizing quality about them, as though all those within its presence were instantly rendered motionless. It bounced off the shards of glass like blue crickets and got caught in the smoke that hung in the air, coating reality with an impenetrable fog, preventing tangibility from merging with the senses. Walking across the battlefield, smelling the acrid stench of gunfire, feeling the crunch of glass underfoot, hearing a baby scream in the background, I was in momentary absentia, limbo personified. Never before had unbelief been so tangible a thing.

A policeman, having holstered his weapon, put a hand on my chest and asked if I was hurt. I shook my head and gently pushed his hand away.

"Officer," I whispered. "I think they shot a waitress in the diner."

I hadn't considered how close Allan and Satí had been to the gunmen. In fact, I hadn't thought about them until that point. I couldn't think straight or fully grasp what had happened until much later. Then I heard her voice, softly at first, like a murmur but rising in alarm as I approached.

"No," she was saying. "No, no, no."

The policeman kept pulling at me as if I owed him money.

"Please, no!" I heard again, louder than before, this time recognizing the voice as Satí's. I'm still unsure why she hadn't called out for help.

The policeman stepped in front of me, shook his head solemnly, but I pushed past him.

"No!" The immediate agony in her voice, even louder than before, tore into my soul. It drove me to tears before I even reached the Toyota.

Satí sat awkwardly hunched over inside the car, whimpering. The driver's side door was slightly ajar, and its window had been shattered. The windscreen was covered with blood and what I assumed was bits of brain matter. Allan's head lay in Satí's lap. She cradled it gingerly as though he was taking a nap.

I wished I could unsee that part of the incident. It was so graphic, so unpleasantly real. I was so overcome with shock that I reached in and shook Allan's leg. His jeans were still warm to the touch. He was there, but he was not. I took hold of his pants in a fist and gave my brother one more tug. He did not recoil. He did not resist. The action offered Satí no comfort. When I pulled back my arm, a sliver of glass cut open my forearm. Though deep, I couldn't remember feeling a thing. My brother's death took precedence.

"Help!" I screamed. "We need help!"

The policeman leaned over, peeked inside the Toyota, and reeled back with a grim expression on his face. He looked towards the flashing red lights at the other end of the parking lot and called for a paramedic, though we both knew nothing would bring Allan back to life.

CHAPTER 3

The trauma of such an incident could derail anyone's life, in part because people perceive things differently, which allows for varied post-tragedy responses. To some, death is a matter of cause and effect. For others, it comes as a severe emotional assault. Even with a group of heartless monsters in one's midst, everyone can sympathize with those who are inexplicably flung into the throes of pain and sorrow. There was little need to detail the sadness which followed for Satí. Once an inviolable personality, she had been rendered frail by consequence.

Satí and Brenda had nothing in common, yet they were the closest friends. Brenda was akin to Thomas Hardy's description of Bathsheba. "*She was of the stuff of which great men's mothers are made. She was indispensable to high generation, hated at tea parties, feared in shops, and loved at crises.*" Sadly, Brenda was nowhere to be seen on the night of the shooting. Satí was stuck with me.

While detectives took statements for their investigation, I distanced myself from the misery for the sake of Satí. I tried to keep an objective view even as matters escalated after the shootout. Allan's red sedan became evidence, so we had to be taken to hospital by ambulance. I received stitches to close the lesion across my forearm. Satí was treated for shock. The doctor gave her a tranquilizer strong enough to dispatch an elephant to dreamland. Around one o' clock the following morning, Satí was released into my care. They stuffed a brown bag filled with medication into my hands and sent us on our way. By means of a stretcher, the ambulance driver and his assistant carried Satí to our spare room and left the house as soon as opportunity presented itself.

Then there was silence. The kind of silence that carried weight and brought discord to one's thoughts. Brenda, aware of what had happened, was booked on the first flight home later that morning. Until then, it was just an unconscious Satí and I in an empty house. The house made no eerie cracks. The wind did not howl outside or beat against the windows. Moscow found solace in our study, curled up in a ball under the desk, something he'd never done before.

For whatever remained of the night, I couldn't sleep. My brain worked like an emotional calculator when confronted with shock. The whole night it kept picking at what had happened, as though it was trying to do the math but couldn't. The harder I tried to decipher events, the more complex the math of it became. I was good with numbers, but the means to rework misery, though no stranger to it, somehow eluded me.

Over the last two years, gang shootouts have become commonplace in our neighbourhood. It had escalated to a level of acceptance. I read about harrowing things in the newspapers, though it had never struck this close to home. It was the type of irony that made me repeat tired clichés like *I never thought it would happen to us*. Yet there we were, in the middle of a modern-day gang turf war, which had now claimed the life of my brother.

Brenda called me before boarding her plane. The flight lasted two hours. I counted down the minutes until her arrival. I made breakfast but couldn't eat. When it was time to collect my wife, I slipped out of the house, leaving the smell of burnt bacon and stale coffee hanging in the kitchen. I hadn't woken Satí. It seemed wiser to let her be.

I returned a short while later with my wife at my side. Satí was sitting on the edge of the bed when we arrived, Moscow purring loudly at her side, gently brushing against her legs. When Satí saw Brenda, she burst into tears. Arms wide, my wife flew into the room. As Brenda entered the room, the door pulled shut of its own accord.

I stood in the empty corridor for a moment, contemplating the shadows that crept across the carpet. The morning sun had found our house once more, attempting to penetrate the melancholy with little success. It had been mere hours since reality had ripped through our lives, though it seemed like days.

I was relieved that Brenda was on the other side of that door. I could be intensely analytical at times. I greeted and treated everyone the same way, even helped elderly people cross busy intersections. Though in danger of being a nice guy, I was not the consoling kind. I never possessed that instinct that formed part of sympathy and reassurance. I did life insurance. I ran the numbers, did the math, planned the budget, highlighted flaws, considered and prepared possibilities, then sold solutions. I had to be cold and emotionless to be effective because my clients only called when someone was either dead or dying. Satí needed Brenda, but Allan, in death, now needed me.

When someone passed away, they became a legal entity on

paper. The paper was divided into two: pluses and minuses. An executor was appointed to calculate the value of the individual's estate by listing assets and liabilities, then to calculate taxes and expedite pay-outs of life policies or savings. As Allan's financial adviser, and appointed executor through my firm, I was intimately aware of his finances. I had revised his entire portfolio the year before. His policies had been structured in such a manner that I formed an integral part of it.

A funeral benefit to one policy paid R 200,000 within twenty-four hours of his death. I was the beneficiary of this amount. It was to cover the funeral and unforeseen costs, like plane tickets for our mother and Satí, should either of them be away at the time. As they were scheduled to do outreach missions in Congo and Zambia later that year, Satí was not named as a beneficiary in his estate. Following an incident in Nigeria where a woman was held hostage until the proceeds of her husband's life policy paid her ransom, I had to restructure his estate so that Satí would never be viewed as collateral through spousal inheritance should they be kidnapped.

All the assets in Allan's estate, about R3 million in policy benefits, would be transferred into a trust. The main members of the trust would be me, Brenda and an accountant chosen by my firm's legal department. The sole purpose of the trust was to fund a suitable lifestyle for Satí for at least ten years. The trust would only be terminated in two instances. Should Satí remarry, the full value of the trust would be paid out to her, and the trust would be deregistered. However, in the unlikely death of Satí, the value of the trust would pay out to us before termination. At their request, I had structured Satí's estate in the exact same way. She had suggested this arrangement, primarily because they had decided never to have children and we were their closest family. As an impartial adviser and neutral overseer of their financial affairs, I had taken direction from them, as well as legal guidance from the non-profit organization that would fund their trips. I was stuck in the middle of something I hadn't been able to predict. Allan's will also stipulated that I had to execute funeral arrangements according to his wishes. Sadly, there was no one more capable of tending to the funeral. I was not equipped to take the reins and lead everyone back to normalcy. I was barely in the right frame of mind to tend to the mountain of financial matters looming over me. Yet, the task of family stalwart now fell on me! The thing which I had greatly feared had come upon me.

And as much as I dreaded the funeral, there was only one thing I dreaded more. The worst part of this ordeal still lay before me, rising from the darkest depths of my loathing like Jacob's ladder and disappearing into the grey depths of the heavens above. I still had to make that terrible phone call. How do you tell a mother that her first-born son had been slaughtered?

CHAPTER 4

Shane interrupted the confused silence with a short cackle. My idea was to pause for effect, but I had drawn it out too long. It had caused a lull. I had to check my timing.

I searched Shane's face for signs of remorse, but only found pleasure instead, as though the thought of having killed someone close to me was giving him a sick kind of joy. There was a hint of uncertainty in his demeanour, which seemed to restrain him. It was difficult not to wish him ill.

Sitting in a room filled with murderers and drug dealers, I was at peace. I was recounting a terrible event, yet I was calm. I was staring at the two people who had been the chief instigators behind my hellish nightmare, but I wished them no harm. Well, not anymore, and not in the way one might naturally want to correct a wrong. Whether because of my erratic reasoning over the last couple of months, or the fact that I had nothing left to lose, my contempt had systematically been replaced by indifference.

"If I knew you would get all that money, I'd have killed him twice." He burst out laughing. Some men in the room, spurred on by his madness, contributed loyal giggles. "I'd kill your whole family for that. Am I right?" he said, winking at Denvor across the room, hoping for some form of validation, but their relationship had clearly soured over the years.

At that moment, Shane's words had the subtlety of a mace tearing through a church choir. I was supposed to have jumped at him and ripped out his larynx with my bare hands, but I had grown tired of my own life and had no intention of confronting him beyond that which I had set in play.

Denvor shot a flash of annoyance, at which Shane appeared to holster his arrogance. Denvor's control had its advantages – and a rather long list of disadvantages.

"I remember that night," said Denvor. He reached for his weapon which lay on the table and slowly spun it around with his index finger, trailing the barrel in a slow arc across the surface. It made a soft grating sound that was hypnotic.

"Yeah, so do I," Shane said coolly, pulling absentmindedly at his jacket zip until it was open. "You were pushing the boundaries out north when we agreed you would stay in Kuils River."

"I told you it wasn't me. It was the crew from Rondebosch," replied Denvor.

"Sure, sure, blame them for everything. Forgiven and forgotten, *tjomma*."

"I'm not your *tjomma*," Denvor said, rising from his chair. "That ship has sailed. And you don't tell me where I must do my business."

Shane's sneer rolled from one side of his face to the other, as though he had trumped Denvor in a word duel. "Put your dummy back. For all we know, this *oke* is rolling with

Rondebosch. Or maybe..." He fired off another suggestive glare at Denvor. "Maybe he's working for you?"

"Stop bullshitting, Shane. If he was working for me, I'd have killed him long ago. If he works for me, then what's the point of all this?"

"I hear you, *tjomma*." Shane refocused his doubts on me. He kicked limply at my chair while scratching his ear. "So, who are you working for?"

Denvor came to my rescue. "You don't sound very sad," he said. "About your brother, I mean."

An image of Allan in his hiking gear flashed inside my mind, hat pulled askew, pushing a path through the greenery. I could recall that day so clearly, our hike around the Silvermine nature reserve in Tokai, the intoxicating aroma of the local shrubbery. It was the day he confided in me about his intentions to ask Satí to marry him. The memory caused my cheeks to bunch up. The skin around my eyes pulled into what felt like crow's feet wrinkles. I knew what that smile on my face looked like. Brenda often told me that a smile was not meant to look depressing. It was my emotional mileage on display, drawn out of me by a clever criminal. This glimmer of sincerity appeared to put Denvor at ease.

"You can't change the past," I replied flatly.

I was dehydrated. Lately, my entire system depended on water to keep going. Without liquids, it was as if my body began to desiccate. My joints stiffened when inactive and the viscosity of my saliva dropped to a sticky consistency that caused my tongue to suck to the roof of my mouth. I took another long sip of water and rolled my tongue around the inside of my cheeks to lubricate it. My lips were cracked, and my head was buzzing again. For a second, I couldn't remember where I had left off. My inability to remember what had happened moments before was slowly getting out of control. Distant memories were instantly accessible, but the last week was a grey area that required effort to unpack.

Shane dropped his act and leaned forward until I could smell the fruitiness of his underarm deodorant waft down from the loosened buttons of his shirt. Watermelon and pineapple, with a hint of coconut. I gagged but covered the repulsion with a sideways cough. He jabbed a finger at me, both eyebrows scrunched up.

"That happened months ago. If the money is in a trust, how's that going to help me?" He cringed, turned to Denvor, and added, "I mean us. Slip of the tongue." He turned back to me, a playfulness turning over on itself as he rolled his murky eyes. "How do we get that money?"

I was about to answer when Denvor spoke up.

"I'm not concerned about the trust, Mr. Gray." Denvor eased into his chair again. "It's unfortunate about your brother. That's the nature of our business. But I'm more concerned about the amount. Three million is south of the amount we were told about. And it still doesn't tell me who you are or who you represent."

"I'm getting to that," I began, adding, "And the name is Gray, just Gray, not Mister."

CHAPTER 5

While Brenda tended to a broken Satí, I stalked into my home office in a sombre state. I should have called my mother with the news while at the hospital. I simply couldn't bring myself to do it. There was no good time to make this type of call, but it was my mother. It was as though I needed time to wrap my head around things. I was about to deliver the harshest blow a mother could receive.

My mother was watching a cooking show when I called. I recognized the tune of the show in the background and caught one or two culinary terms as we spoke. She said she was sitting in front of the television, drinking her first cup of coffee for the morning. Sheba, her half-blind Jack Russell terrier, lay curled up in its basket beside her.

She was happy to hear from me. I could tell. She was chatty, elated. I was looking for an opportunity in the conversation, planning how to break the news to her. She told me about a movie she had watched the night before. Then she stopped short. There was a sudden cold silence.

"What's wrong?" she asked.

"I have some bad news." What a horrible thing to do on a Saturday morning, I thought. I was a terrible son.

"What? What happened?" I could hear her breath, beating weakly against the cellular phone, a slight wheeziness to it.

"It's Allan."

"No," she whispered, to no avail. The horror had been cast in stone. It could not be undone. I wish I could cut out those words and piece together something different, but it was too late. I forged ahead.

"There was a shooting at a restaurant. He was in the car when it happened, protecting Satí. Everything happened so fast."

"My boy, my boy," she whimpered. "Allan …"

"Mom, I'm so sorry. I couldn't…"

I wish I could say tears were welling in my eyes, but I'd be lying. My throat burned and my bottom lip trembled, but the rest of me, nerves and sinews and thoughts, all just froze up inside of my body. I was more touched by the sound of my mother's agony than my brother's death, but I was still stuck with this inability to digest the fullness of it all.

"My boy," she said again, this time with remarked effort.

Then I heard a loud cracking sound as the phone fell to the ground.

I heard the presenter of the cooking show list ingredients in the background, followed by Sheba's soft whimpering and sniffing.

By the time I got an ambulance crew to her house, she was gone. The presiding doctor at the time explained that her heart simply couldn't take the shock. I was told she had died gracefully, falling back into her favourite chair in a seated position, head slumped forward. The ambulance crew said Sheba was resting on her lap like an ewe lamb.

After Allan's death, I had been reluctant to call my mother. Deep down I knew this would happen. I had anticipated that she would shut down when the news found her ears. When her parents had died, she became near catatonic. And when my father had passed away, she just caved in. Her hair went grey within a month. She suffered ongoing heart palpitations ever since. The death of either of her sons would push her over the edge. A wave of emotions had been set in motion long ago, raging in the emptiness of her being, muted only by the possible babble of grandchildren, which would never come. Her turmoil had fallen silent. And my lack of surprise was a consequence of having conditioned myself for the worst outcome.

More and more the week was turning into a Greek tragedy. Without any decent support structure, I realized that our world had been turned upside down. We were alone, having no one to associate with or to lament to. My mother and brother were gone. Brenda's parents had died a couple of years ago. She had no siblings or living relatives. Satí had no one to turn to for emotional support because she had been an only child as well, with no living grandparents. Even poor Sheba had no one to take care of her.

Later that day I drove out to my mother's house in George to collect Sheba while Brenda stayed with Satí. It was a five-hour drive from Cape Town, but with my thoughts in disarray, it felt like five days. It was strange to be in my mother's house without her there. More accurately, it was strange to know that she would not be coming back. She was gone.

I slept in my dead mother's house that Saturday night, enslaved by unfamiliar solemnity, then drove back Sunday morning. I was now obliged to arrange two funerals, simultaneously. I was the last surviving member of my immediate family. I suddenly felt like the decaying branch of a poisoned tree. For the remainder of the weekend, and the following week, I was in a state of confusion. I became a distant machine, not a single clear thought breaching the surface of the shallow pond that made up my consciousness. Was it all a dream? I pondered about the averages for occurrences such as this. I was not looking to break records, but I was curious.

My wife was amazing during this zombie phase where I fast-tracked through the stages of grief. She embraced Sheba as our own while trying to console Satí and running the house. She gauged my various moods as though she was walking around inside my head. It helped that she was a psychology major.

As gingerly as she dealt with me, Brenda was substantially more compassionate with Satí. When the poor soul found out about my mother's passing, she relapsed, so overcome with sorrow that we had to call upon the paper bag pharmacy to tranquilize her. I had considered not telling Satí at all, but as we were planning a joint funeral. I foresaw a loud and public collapse when she finally saw the two coffins being lowered into the ground.

I signed a stack of paperwork, in duplicate, one pile for Allan, the second for my mother. By law, I was required to keep the paperwork for five years. As luck would have it, I had tended to my mother's financial matters as well. I was the only one in the family with an eye for finances. As their intermediary, I was obligated to execute their wills post-haste. My brother had left a small fortune in a trust to provide for Satí. My mother had left us some sentimental items, like her small jewellery collection, and her two-bedroom George townhouse in a small estate along the Garden Route region. Allan and I would share ownership of the house, but her will stipulated that in the event of death, the surviving sibling would enjoy full ownership.

The thought of relocating Satí to my mother's house was an encouraging one. Brenda said it was a bit heartless. For the sake of simplicity, we decided to sell the house immediately. That way we could transfer ownership of the title deed at the point of winding up my mother's estate. It was just a house. The breadth of her entire life, summed up in brick, cement, three suitcase-loads of clothing, and a jewellery box. What would we gain by hanging on to these things?

The funeral was held on a Saturday morning. As anticipated, it was a ghastly affair. My brother's money had paid out in the nick of time. It funded both funerals, with change left over. There were some friends scattered about the pews, neighbours I'd never seen before and a group of people from my mom's old bridge club. The funeral parlour had sent emotive eulogies to local newspapers and designed depressing service leaflets with purple and green flowers arranged around the edges. The pastor gave a sombre sermon that expounded on the sufferings of Job, though the irony of it drowned out the sincerity of the message. I realized my thoughts were a mess when I mounted the small podium. I was not a wordsmith, nor a prolific orator. My incoherent address was my failing ode to the departed. While lacking in sense, at least I was clear and audible.

When Satí decided to share her grief, it was difficult to comprehend what was going on. Between the snot and the tears and the constant wailing, she mumbled through a bastardized version of what sounded like a fable, then recited the lyrics of an old Toni Childs song. She was an absolute wreck, and it pained me to see her that way, writhing about on the apron of the church's stage as though she had caught on fire and was trying to snuff out the flames on her burning limbs. Brenda and I attempted to coax her away from the podium, one on either side whispering words of encouragement into her ears. She kept calling for Allan, blaming God for taking him away too soon. We took turns holding her hand while the other nudged her to one side. This had to look insensitive to other mourners, but she was doing herself more harm by breaking down in public. Her grief needed solitude and time, but she was not granting herself either. We offered her unreserved love and an emotional support system, but we could not offer her the one thing she needed, which was to have Allan returned to her. Nothing less would suffice. I had been dealt double the blow, yet I was seemingly unfazed. I tried not to get stuck on the possibility that my inability to experience loss meant there was something wrong with me.

After the service, we greeted some people then made a hasty exit out the back. I was hooked through a woman's arm on either side, forming a linked chain that made up a morbid trio. We looked like the Three Mourners of Dijon outside the tomb of Philip the Bold, as captured in alabaster by Claus Sluter. We were a pathetic, beautiful sight and everyone who saw us was instantly blasted with a burst of sympathy.

Nearing our car, eager to return home, a slender man stepped out from behind a tree in the churchyard. He approached cautiously.

"Hi there!" he said.

He had a sincere smile, friendly eyes, and an endearing manner.

We stopped and turned to look at him, three vague and unknowing faces. We waited for him to make the first move.

"My name is Malcolm Zedek." We shook hands. "You probably don't remember me."

I frowned and made a vacuous gesture to nudge him along. A sprinkle of rain had followed the service. I thought it unwise to linger about in the cold. The day had also gotten the better of me and I sensed Satí teetering on the brink of another episode. I shook my head when he didn't respond.

"I was your father's legal aid. It's OK, you were just a boy."

"Sorry…" I shook my head again.

"I'm so sorry for your loss. I tried calling but the numbers on file are all disconnected."

"I upgraded a while back." I might have sounded annoyed.

"To avoid a track-and-trace cost, I contacted the mortuary and got the service date. Thought it was better to do this in person."

"To do what?" I held out my arms instinctively, as though shielding Brenda and Satí from an attacker. This display of territorial masculinity was new to me. I had never been so prepared to fight for what was mine, but these two women were all I had left.

"You needn't worry," he said and shuffled backward. "It's nothing untoward. It's a tiny matter of incalculable significance. Perhaps we could meet Monday morning, around ten?"

"Mr. Zedek, your timing is…" I trailed off, studying the frown on my wife's face. She filled me with so much strength and conviction. The sudden humidity had caused her hair to frizz. Tiny drops clung to her fringe like dew to a spider's web. I closed my eyes and pinched the bridge of my nose. "Is it a pressing matter?"

"Very, but it will take mere minutes of your time. I promise."

From experience, I knew that pertinent legal and financial matters seldom took minutes to sort through. Against my will, I acquiesced. I palmed his business card, address on the back. I was unsure how to adjourn the encounter, so I shuffled forward.

"You have my sincerest sympathy. Until Monday." He offered a consoling nod to Brenda and Satí, then disappeared amongst the trees.

I longed to take a leave of absence from work but was unable to. Work matters and personal matters became entwined. Handling both estates resulted in me juggling the roles of financial advisor and husband while fielding Brenda's concern for Satí. I pored over our mother's and Allan's paperwork all weekend to expedite the claims process. First thing Monday, I was outside the Bellville office of Malcolm Zedek.

A fine drizzle cast a haze over the world. It caused the sporadic lights of the morning traffic to flare up with unwanted urgency, filling motorists with irregular panic. The specks of condensation floated down on the fresh steam that rose from the tarred roads, like liquid snowflakes. It was chaos on the roads: honking, screaming, screeching tires, emergency response sirens echoing in the distance. Everything seemed disjointed, out of place, wrought with underlying friction, and bent on maintaining a sense of gloom. It was the world as I knew it, but turned upside down, as though it had become irritable, impatient, and purposely mean.

Zedek greeted me when I stepped off the elevator. His office was on the second floor, at the end of a long, carpeted corridor. My reservations about the meeting wilted away once he led me into his office. Though I was completely spent by this stage, my burden became lighter with every step. I was overcome by indifference. It was a profound experience. It quickly became clear that Zedek was a sage legal adviser who was masterful at working around such delicate issues.

We were alone. In this line of work, there was always a witness present. However, he was utterly at ease and that put me at ease.

His office windows overlooked a large park, a portion of a schoolyard to one side and a clump of trees stretching into the distance, with Brackenfell looming at the outer edges where the trees ended. The rain and the clouds overhead added a certain credence. Nature and youth; new beginnings and all that. I was not prone to sentiment, but as of late, my views on life had taken the road less travelled.

Zedek circled the small Imbuia desk and politely pointed toward the opposite chair.

"Coffee or tea?"

"Neither." I declined.

"Good, because my secretary is on an errand and my coffee-making skills are questionable. Thank you for coming."

"I didn't really have a choice, did I?"

He was taken aback but not offended. He seemed genuinely concerned.

"Sorry, Mr. Zedek. I don't mean to be brusque. This last week feels like a year. I would like to get on with things, then try to scrape my life together."

"I understand. I will be brief." Zedek folded his hands, with long, tapered fingers intertwined. "When your father started working, he created an investment portfolio. He kept it active his whole life and fuelled it with ten percent of his earnings. He carefully adjusted the amount whenever he received increases, bonuses or changed jobs. Whether by fluke or divine insight, his investment options were nothing shy of brilliance. Mostly offshore, iron ore companies, mining giants, and so on. Seemingly safe investments, though not without a bit of risk. His portfolio became a sizable one, and the investments grew exponentially."

I put up a hand to stop him. "Whoa, wait just a minute, will you?" The frowns creasing on my forehead physically hurt. "I don't understand. What investments?"

"Your father's personal investments."

"My father never kept investments."

"I can assure you he did."

My head indicated the negative of its own accord. "That's not possible. How come we never heard of this? I am…" I stopped myself short, shut my eyes in annoyance. "Was. I *was* my mother's financial adviser. I never found any investments when I pulled up my father's profile."

"Yes, about that…" Zedek shuffled papers around, then extended a copy of an old South African Identification document. He shifted his spectacles, gave the document a hard stare, then levelled his eyes at me, smiling. "The inception date was way before he met your mother, which is why your father used his old ID number. It's still the same person, but it was never required to update records. You might say, he slipped through the cracks. It does happen." He cleared his throat and extracted more documents from a yellow manila folder, scrutinizing them mid-air. Outside, a large truck rumbled, the top sections of two shipping containers sailing past the bottom of the window. "Shortly before his death, he changed the beneficiaries of the portfolio. He was adamant that the entire portfolio be encashed when your mother died and be payable to you and your brother. When the coroner submitted your mother's death certificate, our database automatically pulled the file from Home Affairs. We simply followed the instructions. It's all automated digital processes these days."

"I don't…" I smiled, not sure how to digest the incredulity of it all. Zedek leaned back in alarm. "I don't understand this."

"Your father's will is a legally binding document. We were obligated to execute your father's wishes. You can't appeal the finality of an individual's demands."

"I know how a will works, Mr. Zedek. I don't understand how he kept this from all of us."

Zedek unfolded and refolded his hands, then added, almost secretively, "Your mother knew."

"What?"

Zedek gave me a vacant stare.

"She struggled financially for years after he passed away." I continued.

"He wanted to take out a life policy to leave an inheritance for her, but your mother sat in that chair and insisted that he rather increase the premiums of the investment. It seemed to me that your mother was the thrifty one."

I leaned forward, allowing the information to find purchase. This last revelation was a difficult one. The wound of losing my mother, much like my brother, was still tender, even at the distance from which I was experiencing it. I was intrigued, because she had opted to lead a modest life, often calling on us for financial support.

At this point, overcome by all manner of thoughts and

emotions, a singular thought formed inside me. Before I could restrain the thought, it poured over my lips.

"How much? What was his portfolio valued at?"

"After taxes and fees, it should be close to five million, give or take. I must just add that your father's will made no mention of your sister-in-law, and your brother passed away before your mother, so you are the sole beneficiary on file."

"You've got to be kidding me," I mumbled.

I sighed and shook my head, overwhelmed by the news. In one weekend, I had lost my family and simultaneously became a multimillionaire. My world was spinning. When I closed my eyes, the black depths of my mind folded over, as though I was being drawn towards a black hole that had formed at the innermost centre of my being. Gravity disappeared and I was left in a weightless vacuum with nothing but the sound of my own breath rasping in my ears, blotting out the shrill sound of children playing in the schoolyard across the road. I was nauseous and my head was throbbing. I thought a vein was about to pop behind my eyes. When I opened my eyes, Zedek stood next to my chair holding out a glass of water in one hand. I'm not sure how much time I lost, but Zedek's confused expression suggested it had been noteworthy.

"You are taking this rather well," he said softly.

"This is madness," I whispered. "What must I do with all that money?"

"Your father had only one request: that you spend it."

"What does that mean?"

Zedek said nothing.

For the next thirty minutes I signed documents, then left in a daze. I saw tiny white spots everywhere, which really freaked me out. They were scattered across the grey flower patterns of the wallpaper in the corridor, like three-dimensional paint splatter. When I got to the car, I was burning to call Brenda with the news, but my fingers were so jittery that I couldn't find her in my contact list. I decided to wait until we could talk face to face. I found it reassuring to sit around a table with my wife and to discuss things. Five minutes of face time usually consolidated our different perspectives on a matter. I knew, now more than ever before, we had to make decisions together.

As a couple we have often played the what-if-I-won-the-lotto game. It seemed like such a harmless game. Now the what-if game had been given a violent shove towards reality – and I had no idea what to do. Brenda and I had to consider all the consequences   carefully.

CHAPTER 6

That night, my wife and I had an uncomfortable discussion about my father's small treasure, not to mention the proceeds from my mother's and my brother's respective estates.

We ate a well-prepared chicken lasagne I had bought on the way back. Satí excused herself after two bites. As she left, a heaviness left the room with her.

We finished pecking at our food and moved to the living room, where the fresh evening air poured in through the open side door. Outside, the sun had drowned in the sea of mountains which lay in the distance. The first stars speckled the blanket of night. The chirping of crickets and the croaking of frogs began to echo across our backyard, adding a pleasant hum to an otherwise depressing conversation between husband and wife.

After I had told her about the type of money we could expect from these three sources of insurance payouts, we sat looking at each other for the longest time, neither of us able to comment, yet confounded by how much our lives had been altered. What would we do with all that money? We were not obliged to do something with the money but forgetting about it wouldn't make it disappear. Would we leave it in a trust for our old age? Reinvest it for greater returns? Give it away to non-profits? Or spend it haphazardly?

Brenda played with her hair, a finger absently tugging at a loose strand as though it was a source of inspiration. Her eyes were distant. Her lip was curled slightly to one side. I had become so accustomed to reading Brenda's every mood. At times she was an open book only to me. She spoke with me without having to utter a single word. Much like a wick led a flame through a candle's wax, she would guide me through her mind without opening her lips. But that evening, as we sat studying each other, our body language was an incoherent jumble of twitches and shrugs. We were unfamiliar with each other. We were strangers. Nothing had prepared us for this influx of wealth. I have worked with finances long enough to know that in the wake of abundance, misery followed. I didn't want that for us. I needed Brenda, and I had no reason to believe that she thought favourably about life without me in it. I imagined us both on a rickety wooden footbridge suspended over a great chasm, hungry wolves guarding both exit points, their growls taunting us.

We found a tiny kernel of comfort in simply letting things be for the immediate future, to not focus on money and to live as though nothing had changed. I put my arm around her, pulled her close until I could smell her life close to my chest and kissed her forehead.

"Let's not lose sight of what's important," she said. It sounded more like a question.

"You and me, babe," I agreed. "Nothing else matters."

With our lives alternating between elation and agony, we were caught in a dangerous trap, which made us blissfully unaware of the imminent danger lurking in our midst. On one side, we were dealing with the emotional consequences of loss. On the other, we were confronted by an instant monetary gain, which offered the ill-timed high of knowing that we would probably never have to work again. What made the situation a metaphorical trap was the very person who would trigger the mechanism, causing the jagged jaws to slam shut on our lives. I have spent hours contemplating how I could have prevented the horror that was about to befall us, but everything happened beyond my sphere of influence.

Brenda had work matters to tend to. As a legal secretary, she had certain obligations that could not be offloaded to more junior team members. I had paperwork to sort through, mostly resulting from the dual tragedies. I lost myself in work, though not to avoid the weight of reality. This was my way of coping, allowing dust to settle and life to marinate. I was a numbers guy – and numbers calmed me.

During this time of busying ourselves, Satí was facing an absolute maelstrom of emotions swirling around in her veins, festering and morphing into something unrecognizable. She had so much pain and sadness that she was like a flower of destruction on the cusp of blooming. Considering the aftermath, her motives were not only questionable but resolute. God alone knew what was happening inside of her.

The day that our little snow globe received yet another violent shake came mere days after my visit to Malcolm Zedek and started like any other. Brenda and I prepared for work. We sat down for breakfast, Satí joining us as another member of our family. We had accepted her presence in our house. She was family. Most of the time she was in her room reading or just staring at the walls. At times she would burst out crying when something stirred a memory of Allan, then I would vacate the room while Brenda did what came naturally to her.

That morning, Satí seemed better than normal. She had a faint smile on her face, which brought out her more prominent features. Her Indian ancestry brought a flair and a grace to her demeanour, which had been absent in her mourning. She proposed a movie night. We were a bit surprised given the previous attempt at a movie night but saw it as a step towards recovery. Later I would retrace her movements and find that she had been as methodical as ever. I spent days gathering information and eventually pieced everything together in the following way.

Satí went about her day with a fresh purpose that would have been admirable had it not been fuelled by grief. After we left, she finished her breakfast, washed dishes, took a long shower, then dressed comfortably in a long summer dress with orange flowers. She locked up, left a note for us on the kitchen island, and went to the garage. That would have been the first time she had been to their car since Allan had been shot. We had planned to sell it but hadn't got around to it yet. I suspect she had lost control over her bladder shortly after getting into the car, because evidence suggests that she deactivated the house alarm minutes later, went back inside, and showered again, leaving her summer dress in the bathtub, where we found it later that evening, drenched in urine. She evidently redressed, in jeans this time, and put a couple of newspapers on the driver's seat to prevent the urine from seeping through. She activated the house alarm once more and off she went.

According to the insurance company's vehicle tracking

reports, she stopped at an ATM, where the surveillance cameras showed her withdrawing a large sum of money, then placed the notes in an envelope she had probably removed from my study. Her routine was varied and slow. Wherever she parked, she remained for a while longer than required. I'd like to think she was systematically replaying the events that unfolded the Friday night her life shattered, but that would be wild speculation on my part. Whatever she was doing to fuel her pain, it created little grey spots on her journey that the car tracker and her credit card couldn't explain.

As she drove about, she went from suburbs to slums. She had spent most of her time in dangerous neighbourhoods, helping drug addicts and street kids find their place in the world. She had tasked herself with helping the troubled and the fatherless. Her roads always led to dark corners, where she served as the light to those in need, but this time her visit was more complex.

I later retraced the route as recorded by the car tracking device, simply because I had difficulty digesting what had happened. The numbers didn't add up. I had to understand why. The directions from the tracker took me through deserted streets and slums where broken bottles were strewn across pavements. At one point, it showed that she parked near the entrance to a block of flats. The building looked dilapidated to me, but this was where she had parked her car. Flaking paint, broken windows, weeds sprouting from cracks in the pavements, faded hopscotch blocks, police sirens a couple of streets over. From what I knew about Satí, this cruel place, the battlefield between compassion and hate, was her office where she fought daily to win the minds and souls of South African youth. Satí, the front-line warrior.

Youth councillors imparted wisdom, nurtured with love,

instilled hope, and inspired with joy. It was a thankless, fruitless occupation, one without a lucrative retirement plan. But the good far outweighed the bad. Allan once told me that educating impressionable minds while impacting and altering the perception of another human being was intoxicating. The drug of affecting real positive change in a young mind was akin to leaving a legacy, which is probably why they had never felt the need to have children, and why, with Satí's life and her spirit in bits, it was apparent that no one could offer guidance to the guide.

The municipal camera systems, a new crime-deterring initiative, clearly showed Satí entering the building that morning. In the footage, a group of wayward teens watched her from the corner, not surprised by her presence there. She was out of shot for a couple of minutes, then returned to her car, where she sat motionless. A thin teenage boy approached the car with a brown paper bag partially concealed under his shirt. He had a shiny, youthful face, big inquisitive eyes, and a tiny mouth. The police identified the boy as Tyron, one of the children Satí ministered to.

In the footage, Tyron stood next to the car for a while, unaware that he was being recorded. His movements suggested that he was reluctant to hand the paper bag, but she clearly had plans, and the bag formed part of it. At one stage, Satí reached out and snatched the bag from the boy, who was shaking his head and pleading with her.

A detective, along with an appointed social worker, interrogated Tyron for hours on end. I read the reports, and it was vague. Tyron went on for a long time about his mother puffing on a crack pipe and how hard it was to live in their neighbourhood. The drinking, the noise, the fighting, the drugs, and so on. After the detective had tired the boy out, Tyron explained what had happened. Apparently Satí had come to his apartment and handed him the money. He instructed her to wait in the car. He told the two interrogators how he ran up the stairs and exited onto the rooftop. From there he ran the length of the roof until he got to a wooden ladder, which acted as a bridge from one roof to the other. He scampered across the wood to the block of flats adjacent to his. He claimed he went down two floors and exited into a communal area, where another boy of about nine waited for him. Tyron remembered how the boy's head had been shaved into a Mohawk hairstyle, then bleached white. This boy called for someone called Malique. A large man appeared on the balcony, his big arms covered in tattoos, from shoulder to wrist. Tyron enacted how Malique narrowed his mean eyes and then how the man eased up once he opened the envelope and fingered through the notes. Tyron tossed the envelope to the boy. Malique then nodded at another boy on the opposite balcony. Tyron said he only saw two murky eyes and an outstretched arm clasping a paper bag. The bag was released, then Tyron caught it with both hands. He made his way back across the roof and took the bag down to Satí. The police raided the block of flats the following day. I was told the courtyard looked exactly as Tyron had described it, but Malique had disappeared off the face of the earth. Of course, the other tenants had never heard of him. Cell phone reports of the communication between Satí and Tyron, revealed how she had pestered the boy. I recalled telling Brenda how it bothered me that Satí was always on her phone, even during suppertime.

From Tyron's apartment, the car tracker showed that Satí

drove back to town at a sedate pace, adhering to the speed limit. She went to a coffee shop some distance from our house and had a light lunch. According to the waiter, she ordered a second cup of coffee and gave a handsome tip, paying by card. Back in the car, Satí drove to where it had all gone astray. She parked the car in the same spot it had been parked that disastrous Friday night. Since the shootout, the restaurant had refurbished its salad bar and installed security cameras. While insightful, it would not prevent misery from occurring twice in one setting.

At first, the police were reluctant to show me the footage, but I threatened them with legal action until they relented. While disturbing to watch, the finality of it all afforded me a strange type of closure.

The cameras that were situated over the entrance had a clear view of Satí in the driver's seat. In the recording, she sat and watched a young couple enter the eatery. The two lovers were holding hands, stealing coy looks at each other, unaware of the world around them. Her eyes scanned over the patrons in the diner, then the children in the outside play area. There was a large tree in the field next to the restaurant. Having been there at that time of day, I could almost hear the comforting sound of the birds chirping as they played in the branches.

For long after, I replayed the footage in my mind to figure out what she must have been thinking about. She sat there for a long time, staring out at the people in the parking area. I firmly believe Satí was looking for something to hinder her plans, a chink in the armour, a tear in the fabric. Alas, she was suffocated by the surrounding happiness. No matter what she saw that day, it would have been insufficient.

She rummaged through her handbag and removed her purse.

Even in the small image, I could tell her hands were trembling as she struggled to find the small picture of Allan in her purse. She pushed her bag aside and held the photo with both hands outstretched over the steering wheel.

After a while, she removed the snub-nosed revolver from the paper bag. There was no evidence that she had used a weapon before that day. It was not a thing of science, though. The footage showed her inspecting the revolving cylinder, tiny dots of the bullets visible in every hole. She slipped the safety catch off, cocked the hammer back with difficulty, then, in keeping with the ancient Indian custom of suttee, she looked down at the photo of Allan, pressed the barrel of the handgun into her mouth at an upward angle and pulled the trigger.

And so ended the life of Satí, abrupt and undignified. It was a tragedy comparable to any tale of woe ever recorded, minus the poison and modernized with a handgun. So brutal. I instantly regretted having insisted on watching the footage. Hard as I tried, I could not unsee it.

I replayed all my interactions with Satí after our lives had been thrown together. I searched for an inception point, a time when she had decided her own fate. However, I couldn't venture back to where we had contributed to her decision-making. There was nothing that could have prevented the outcome. Unlike the Biblical tale of the widow of Nain who had lost her son, I could not raise Allan from the dead, so she had decided to join him in death. And that was that.

CHAPTER 7

I looked around the room where I was being held. Held was not the correct word. I was there willingly. Well, not entirely of my own free will, but I had planned the encounter with my captors. Then again, was it a plan if it had been arranged while you were technically absent?

The room seemed prepped for torture or interrogative purposes. It was larger than I had imagined. Maybe because the only furniture was a table and three garden chairs. There were white strips of plaster where cracks had been filled up, curling along the walls like a pair of writhing snakes sailing across the plaster.

The house was nestled in the rounding of a cul-de-sac. Viewed from outside the house was a light brown block with dark brown trim; double-storied, double garage, covered entranceway, and a tall chimney extending above the pitched roof, slightly off-centre. It blended with the other houses in Highbury, one of the suburban hubs of Kuils River. With its matching paving and uniform chest-high corrugated fencing, the house appeared to adhere to an unwritten guideline that the whole street had to maintain. The three black SUVs in the driveway, with tinted windows and shiny spinner rims, as well as the four tattooed henchmen on the front porch, cast a stain on the notion of normalcy. If that didn't do the trick, the sight of me being hauled from the boot of a black sedan, hands tied and gray sock covering my head, would have given the street something to talk about.

The house looked incomplete and semi-furnished, partly because it was trapped in an occupational limbo. There were no plants, fancy decorations, or picture frames on the walls. It was void of memories because it had recently changed owners. A house, not yet a home. I remembered studying the house from the outside when I had still been bent on killing Denvor. I would sit in my car with binoculars, looking for a way in, but he had only purchased it months before on auction, along with some of the other houses in the street. His drug money had aided him with the transition from slums resident to suburb landlord. At the time, he was fitting a security system and motion cameras to the new house, while his family stayed at their other house. It was a funny thing, this gangster business. Yet, as with all walks of life, that which one treasured most, one protected.

The turf war between Shane and Denvor had dealt them both serious financial blows and it had sparked interest from competitors in central Cape Town and further afield, as well as the police. Though both drug bosses were living in style, they couldn't retire at will. They needed this life to survive. With these two I have found that money was constantly tied up in something or in some manner running away from them. I was told that while they had been partners, they had been an unstoppable force that kept challengers at bay. However, an underlying tension kept pulling them apart. As an amateur sleuth, I was able to uncover the cause of their split: Macky. Shane's brother, Macky, a menace to all who knew him, had confronted Denvor numerous times and made subsequent advances on his wife, Tamara. Denvor had few weaknesses, but his family and his pride were the two that haunted him endlessly. Macky had stirred the pot once too often and eventually his brother paid the price. Following a near-fatal run-in with Denvor, Shane suggested the two part ways indefinitely. And so they had, to their own disdain.

There were twelve men in the room, most of whom I had crossed paths with during the last couple of months. There was no prevalent nationality present, just a bunch of violent, fatherless, grey-faced boys in young men's bodies. They all formed part of one body – they were the gang. Even as the two bosses sat opposite each other, the men in the room were jumbled about, loyal only when told to be so. They stood around in small groups along the walls, friends-turned-enemies, now uncertain companions during this interrogation, their interests momentarily aligned.

I sat staring at the table for a while. I could feel that awkward smile on my face. Thinking about my father's secret millions always brought that desperate horror upon my features. The smile presently faded away as a burst of memories blew through the empty corridors of my mind. I saw my father sitting at a picnic table with me on his lap, spreading coins out over the coarse wooden surface. He turned the coins over with his long fingers, counting out the change to buy me a toasted sandwich. I saw my brother's broken head resting in Satí's lap. I saw my mother slumped over in her chair, head lolling sideways in an eternal state of slumber as rigor mortis set in. These memory dumps came and went and often left me semi-catatonic for a few minutes. I had no control over them anymore. When they arrived, I obliged and let them play all the way through.

Denvor shifted uneasily in the shadows, scratched at something on the table with one nail.

"Malique?" he said loudly.

At the outermost part of the circle of men, stood the formidable figure of Malique. He shrugged sheepishly and pouted his lips.

"Explain," Denvor demanded in a reserved manner.

"The lady wanted a gun, Denvor. I sold her the gun. I don't ask what they want it for."

Malique's voice betrayed his nervousness. He stood erect, hands clasped behind his back, like a soldier addressing a superior.

Denvor nodded, lost in thought. He began pushing and pulling the tip of his index finger along the length of his nose. He closed his eyes for a couple of seconds and sighed.

"That's quite a story," he said finally.

"Probably all lies," Shane interjected. "There's no money, is there?" He looked genuinely amused. "Come on, be honest, you're having a piss? This is all a game, right?"

I giggled, more by accident than intent, another side effect of the memory dumps. "That's exactly what the investigator said."

"Investigator?" Shane jumped up as though I'd thrown my empty water bottle at him. "What investigator? Police?"

Shane was naturally quick to anger, but doubly so when cops were involved. He had been bred that way. An abusive father, a drug addict for a mother, and a vindictive brother had left him with few alternatives. He lived by one rule: eat or be eaten. In his world, there was no grey area, no chance to blink. He never waited for an opportunity to present itself. He simply latched on when the move suited his lunacy, and he didn't let go until he got what he wanted. He was cruel, manipulative, violent, and just shy of being stupid. He would die young, and I suspected he was aware of it. Strange as it seemed, he feared only one thing, and that was going to jail. He randomly inspected his runners for wires and distanced himself from operations to limit his involvement. Those who lived without care often had one solitary care that dominated their nightmares. To Shane, the smell of jail food and the steel of prison bars served as grim reminders of his sinful life.

He pushed his chair back, sat up straight and glanced out the windows. "Do the coppers know you're here?"

I snorted. "Police? I wish!"

"Cops?" Shane gave Denvor a quick flash of distress and distrust. "You hear that? The *bra*'s been dealing with coppers. Did anyone check this *bra* for a wire yet?"

I'd anticipated his paranoia. In fact, I'd been waiting for it to show face.

"The cops were useless. They came around after my mother died. Detectives, two of them. They asked questions. I told them what I saw. They took notes. Then they left. Satí also gave them clear descriptions of you two, but the investigation stalled. All promises, no arrests."

Shane smirked, savouring the idea that the police could be that inadequate.

"If the cops did nothing, then what investigator are you talking about?" Denvor cut in.

"The claims investigator," I said matter-of-factly. "He took an unhealthy interest in my affairs."

CHAPTER 8

As Satí set herself free from her prison of memories, she imprisoned us with an additional revenue stream. Her life insurance, much like my brother's life insurance, had me listed as the beneficiary in the event of Allan's death. There had been additional investments Satí had forgotten about. These had grown substantially over the last five years and had a protector benefit that would surrender a staggering capital amount in the event of death. The whole matter had become incredibly complex and distressing. As a numbers guy, even I had trouble keeping up with everything.

Then there was Satí's funeral. Undoubtedly the most forgettable event I ever had the misfortune of attending. The memory of it still haunts me. She had taken her life that Wednesday, so we arranged the funeral for Saturday morning, which would be precisely one week after laying my mother and Allen to rest, and two weeks after the shootout at the restaurant. Because of the unique nature and extent of the tragedy, Brenda was released from work obligations. In planning her funeral, we realized there was no one to invite. Satí's life had revolved around

Allan, so we invited the same people we had invited to Allan's funeral. Those who had attended the first funeral simply couldn't bear another one. They were either too shocked and dismayed to RSVP, or they were hoping to avoid it altogether. We called some of them as the day drew nearer, but were met with unanswered rings, endless sobs, or a barrage of apologies. Consequently, no one pitched on the day. Not even fellow teachers who had been dear friends to Allan and Satí. At one stage, I suggested hiring a funeral party since money wasn't a problem, but Brenda insisted that it would sour the already sombre occasion. I just wanted it over.

That Saturday was a blisteringly hot day. So hot that I could feel perspiration accumulating around my collar and my cuffs, drenching my grey socks. When a hint of a breeze snuck through the graveyard, bouncing along the tombstones like a wandering soul, I pulled my collar away to scoop air into my body. To one side of the gravesite stood a tall, lonely river bushwillow tree. Its pale grey branches hung as though in salute, not a single leaf aflutter, casting a low shadow that seemed to peek into the hole where the coffin was destined to be lowered into. There we stood: a tired-looking weekend pastor with hollow features and deep-set eyes, Brenda, and me. We had decided to forego the traditional church service and rather do a dedication by gravesite. I was anxious and fidgety throughout the pastor's sermon. It felt as though a giant hand was closing around my chest and my arms, squeezing me. Loosening my tie didn't alleviate the pressure. I wanted to scream at the tree and run through the graveyard with my hands in the air. Earlier that week, as Satí had taken her own life, a severe headache had started up somewhere behind my eyes. I was a migraine sufferer, so headaches and tension pains were not new to me. However, this had been something else. The pain had arrived as Satí departed – and it never really went away after the funeral.

In the coming weeks, money began pouring in from all sources. The first monies to arrive were funeral benefits or final expenses. While it was cruel to think of financial matters in this way, Satí's death actually expedited the winding up of Allan's estate and the need for a trust in his name, as well as her own. As with Allan's insurance, he had been listed as her spousal beneficiary, and in the event of his death, I was the next of kin. The death of Satí resulted in the deregistering of the trust I had created for Allan's estate, prior to the estate even being wound up. With neither Satí nor Allan, there was no need to establish a trust, which meant the lump sum covering the amounts of both policies would be paid out directly to me. This process was alarmingly straightforward. The proceeds from my father's secret investment portfolio were similarly uncomplicated. His investment assets were encashed, taxed within the funds, and paid over to me. My mother's house was sold while in the estate, though the asset couldn't be prematurely monetized. As there were no suspensive conditions provided for by the master of the court, the estate agent who had sold her house kept the deeds office on standby until the estate had been properly wound up. Once the estate had been concluded, the title deed was transferred from my mother to me, and immediately to the new owners. The purchase amount would be paid out directly to me.

Three of my closest family members passed away within a two-week period and I received millions of Rands as compensation for my loss. It was a fascinating nightmare. Brenda and I had gone from secretly anxious to being cold and despondent at regular intervals. I was standing at the edge of a precipice. The long drop into darkness seemed inviting. If it hadn't been for Brenda, I would have done something terrible. She was my anchor, my sanity. Throughout the whole debacle, I hadn't shed a tear. At times I wondered whether I was incapable of experiencing emotions. These fears were dispelled every time I rested my head on Brenda's lap or held her in my arms. My love for her at that specific time of my life outweighed all the gold in the world. She was by true North, my reason for living.

Shortly after the funeral, Brenda gave notice at her firm. There was no need for her to continue working. I knew her bosses would never find another Brenda, but neither would I, and I needed her more than they ever would. With death all around us, I found a renewed appreciation for her. If there was a singular positive consequence that spawned forth from Sati's demise, it was how we decided to push everything aside and draw even closer to each other.

The detectives dropped by, the same two as before, in part to pay their respects, but also to investigate our roles in Sati's suicide, and in greater part to find out what we intended to do with the car since it now formed part of two separate investigations. What use did we have for the vehicle? We could buy imported sports cars without breaking a sweat.

A week or two after Sati's funeral, the claims investigator first came into our lives. He arrived the same way winter did, with an unexpected chill that crawled up my spine. There was no way to be brief about this man.

In the finance industry, there was a strange occurrence when claims were paid out. Since the dawn of the digital age, information has become accessible to all who had need of it.

Everything was recorded. Masses of people were employed to analyse whatever the supercomputers and systems flagged as worthy of suspicion. When a person received multiple inheritance settlements it could raise a red flag, following which an independent investigation would ensue. This exercise was usually conducted by an insurance or claims investigator, an internal or private finance detective who pursued a particular financial institution's interest. Since my scenario had affected policies and investments across multiple institutions, it had probably caused a large magnifying glass to be cast over my life and my finances.

The investigator tasked with finding the flaw in my presumably nefarious plans was a man named Bertie September.

I first met him in my yard one morning; the same way one might discover an abandoned puppy on the sidewalk. I was on my way out to finalize documentation when I came upon this strange man, standing inside the property, studying our lawn. He was an obscure little man, with broad shoulders and an awkward paunch. He wore a dull brown suit and carried an old leather satchel that looked similar to the one that belonged to my father, which he clasped behind his back as he leaned over to inspect our grass and our flowers.

"Such pretty marigolds," he said with a slight stutter.

I was strangely bemused by his demeanour, but once his beady eyes met mine, I felt a brief shiver travel up my leg. My ever-present headache intensified, and those little white spots resprinkled my periphery.

"It's just grass," I said, sensing his eyes on my frowning features.

"I mean there, by your bedroom window," he said as he

waddled his way up the narrow path towards me.

"How do you know that's our bedroom?" I asked.

He smiled.

"Is it not your bedroom?" His soft half-stutter annoyed me tremendously.

I looked around the yard to see if there was anyone else to direct my question to. "I'm sorry, but who the hell are you?" I asked. "And what are doing on my property?"

"You have a rent-to-own agreement in place with the landlord, but..." he stopped to push his glasses back with one finger, then continued, "...but it's not really your property yet, is it?"

"Our agreement substitutes a basic rental agreement, which entitles me to the right to privacy and admission. Now who *are* you?"

He smiled as though he had conceded a point in a game of squash.

"My name is Bertie September," he said and extended a shaky hand.

I shook hands, and added, "September? It's almost your month." He didn't find that funny.

"Ah, indeed." He pushed his spectacles back again and refocused his beady eyes. "I wonder if you could spare me a minute?"

"I was on my way out."

"I won't be long. It's regarding some policies and investments that have come under scrutiny. I'm the appointed claims investigator."

I looked at my watch and sighed. "I can give you the length of a cup of tea?"

"That is just fine," he said and forced a smile.

He walked about the living room while I made tea. I kept a wary eye on him from the kitchen. When Bertie saw Sheba lying in her bed near the side door, he seemed visibly repulsed. He kept a hand over his nose as though the old dog was a salmonellosis carrier, and he would contract something if he came too close to it. I quickly took some painkillers for my headache, then carried in tea and biscuits on a tray. Brenda was out, so I tried my best to be hospitable. It backfired.

"Tea," I said to the cup as I pushed the tray closer to the stranger, "Meet Bertie."

He smiled pleasantly, but the cup of tea trembled cautiously as it slid across the surface of the small table. Bertie added half a spoon of sugar, a drop of milk, then did the strangest thing. He dipped a finger into the cup and carefully licked it off as though he was devouring a delicacy.

"Lovely," he said. He wiped his finger with a napkin and never touched the cup again.

He removed a file from his satchel and paged through it with intentional slowness. What followed was an uncomfortable bit of dialogue. I was asked about my family and their policies, which hinted at the possibility that I was suspected of committing insurance fraud. He admitted to having interviewed police about Sati's suicide but still questioned me in a manner befitting an interrogation. His questions were repetitive, with only subtle changes, as though he was trying to catch me in a lie. As he pressed on, my headache became unbearable. At times he stared into my soul, not looking away long enough for me to swallow my spit. It was exasperating to feel so judged without someone uttering a single word of judgement. He left after about thirty minutes; by then my annoyance had transformed into a sarcastic grin.

That was not the last I would see of Bertie September.

CHAPTER 9

Brenda allowed me a lot of space to tend to legal and financial matters, in part because she knew there was a lot more at play than just the mountain of paperwork on my desk. Every piece of paper filed, signed, or documented was an uncomfortable memory or gray area dealt with. I was facing my grief the only way I knew how, by working through the numbers that lay in front of me.

One Monday evening, sitting in my home office, I reached a point where the end was in sight. Cold air had snuck into the room while I was poring over the documentation and curled around my ankles like a frigid snake. I slowly pushed back my roller chair, the wheels grinding over the tiles. I heard joints crack as I stretched out my legs and arms. I leaned into the chair, yawned, and studied the desk from an elevated point that felt like another world.

On either side of my glowing laptop screen were two stacks of papers and files. Collectively, they were the four pillars of numbers and words that made up the remains of Allan, my mother, my father, and Satí. In compiled paper, the quietus of each was more final than the sight of a coffin descending into a hole in the earth. I turned my laptop screen down and switched off the light as I left the room.

There was an eerie silence in the house, drifting through the corners and around the bends as though it was a vagrant lost in the wrong house. I found Brenda asleep on the couch, her head sunken into a couch pillow, hair flattened on one side, and her lips pulled askew so that they revealed a couple of her teeth. Her cheek was flushed with sleep and, as I watched, her eye twitched thrice, in quick succession. I removed a fleece blanket from below the coffee table and unfurled it over her body.

I sat down on the mohair rug and stretched my stockinged feet out until the tips of my toes touched the bottom of the coffee table. I rested my back against the couch and folded my arms. I was close enough to hear Brenda's breathing in my ears, close enough to take in the distinctive smell of her body mingling with the soft scent of her perfume. Her warmth radiated over my back and my head.

My mind drifted and a deluge of emotions poured through me. I did not shiver or whimper or sniff or heave or moan; nor did I compress my chest as one would when the physical act of crying had its way. Tears simply rolled down my cheeks with no effort on my part. It was not a display of stoicism. It was just raw emotions.

Somewhere in the night, we found our way to the bedroom, where she lay in my arms until the first bits of sun appeared on the curtains, bleeding outward as the morning settled over our house.

A visible elation unfolded inside Brenda's being when I revealed that the documentation had been done. She put her arms around me and pushed her lips into the base of my neck.

"I'm so glad," she whispered. "It's finally over."

We had coffee together, then showered and got dressed. I had to go to the office to submit the documents and to tend to other business. The world kept turning. My misfortune was not enough to send it spiralling off its axis. My clients, though few, still had matters that needed my attention. I'd neglected them plenty. Though I had communicated the circumstances of my absence, I couldn't delay their queries indefinitely. I never had to explain my desire to return to work, the absurd need to keep my mind occupied. My wife understood.

A representative from the funeral home had called us the week before. The city morgue had forwarded Sati's personal belongings to them and they were eager to offload the goods to us. Brenda, having freed herself from her work faster than anticipated, offered to run our errands. She would drop off a final document at the offices of Zedek & Co., then head to the funeral home to collect the effects they kept for us.

At my office, I was either showered with sympathy or people avoided me in my misery, afraid they would catch it themselves. I moved about the corridors like a shadow; there one moment, gone the next. I wanted to move on with life. The best way to do that was to focus on work.

Brenda left Zedek's office in our grey Audi sedan. According to the car tracking device and witnesses, she kept to the speed limit on the road back from Bellville to the morgue in Durbanville, where she collected Sati's wedding ring, bracelet, pocket pen, and purse, all items that had been on her corpse.

Brenda returned to Belville via Old Oak Boulevard. She drew up to a red light at the intersection of Old Oak and Old Paarl.

Dash cam footage from the car behind Brenda showed that she was still slowing down when a blue Volkswagen Golf with tinted windows blared passed, nearly pushing her off the road. The Golf cut in front of her and mounted a curb, its backside bouncing and screeching across the island separating her lane from oncoming traffic. The vehicle raced along the narrow island, scraping another car in the process, cut down the pole upholding the horizontally mounted traffic light with a plonking sound. It swerved back around a little green Daihatsu halted at the light and ploughed forward into the traffic that zipped through the intersection. It first struck an SUV coming from the right, was flung outward by the force, then struck a BMW which came from the left. What followed was a chain of accidents, about three cars a side smacking into others until there was a pile-up and the flow of cars bottlenecked, followed by screams and a lonely car horn blaring off to one side.

The blue Golf, the instigating force behind the mess of mangled metal, came to a standstill on the curb of the island, its front grille facing the opposing intersection from where it had entered. Traffic cameras overlooking the intersection showed three or four brave souls exiting their vehicles and surveying the scene. They went from car to car to see if anyone needed help. Brenda, being one of them, approached the green Daihatsu which had been scraped by the Golf.

Brenda stepped down from the centre island and peered into the car. A woman named Wendy Makeba sat motionless in her car, eyes transfixed on the chaos in front of her, both hands clasping the steering wheel. Her little toddler was screaming in the back seat. She later confided in me that the memory of being frozen and unable to tend to her child was surreal to her. Wendy explained to me how Brenda reached into her car, touched her face, and tilted her head, forcing her to make eye contact. She told Wendy not to worry, to take care of her little one. Reality slowly unfolded in front of Wendy's eyes. She reached into the back seat, unbuckled little Themba from his baby chair and took him into her arms. She nodded absently at Brenda. From her vantage point, Wendy could see Brenda entering the ring of mayhem where car parts and debris filled the intersection.

Brenda went over to the SUV, sidestepping a twisted bumper that lay in front of Wendy's Daihatsu. The SUV had succumbed to the impact. Its nose had crumpled in on the driver's side where it had struck the Golf. Witnesses said the engine hissed, like a horse ridden to collapse. Brenda leaned in to help the driver regain consciousness. She pulled at the door, but it had been folded inward by the impact. She went around and opened the passenger door. She kept at it until the man came to, his eyes rolling from side to side. Wendy described the driver as a burly man with long hair, blood pouring from his nose.

While Brenda was inside the SUV, more people crept from their vehicles and began milling about the scene. The BMW, the Golf's second victim, had skidded across the road, leaving a black semi-circle of tire residue in its wake. Its front had been ripped open and curled over to one side. The driver was a young man with silky blonde hair, as was visible on the outer edge of the traffic cam footage. He didn't appear to have a scratch on him. His face was ashen and his eyes gaunt.

Brenda left the driver of the SUV and made her way across the intersection. She skipped over to the BMW. The owner seemed unresponsive at first but later nodded absently that he was fine.

Behind Brenda, the driver's side door of the blue Golf shuddered and parted. Trying to shush her boy, Wendy could make out a figure exiting the wrecked car. At the time, she had felt no resentment towards the driver of the Golf. Like everyone present, she knew the car had caused the accident; however, she hadn't been afforded the luxury of reworking the information. For no reason other than curiosity, she looked at the man spilling out of the wrecked car.

He crawled across the pavement, then struggled to his feet. He stood next to the Golf for a long time, gathering himself, hunched over, hand outstretched to steady himself. One shirt sleeve had been torn open, with blood flowing from his shoulder down his arm and dripping from the barrel of the gun in his hand. As the sound of sirens drew nearer, the man on the screen became visibly alert. He shook his head, tried to walk, but stumbled and tipped over to one side, slamming against the side of his car. He steadied himself once more, lifted his weapon and took aim at Wendy's car on the opposite side of the intersection. A surge of adrenaline blew into her veins when she realized the danger. She gasped and shifted her boy to one side. She tugged frantically at the door lever, but the car was locked. The gunman, swaying from side to side, shifted the gun's barrel from her Daihatsu to the SUV, then back again, as though searching for a target.

At that point a police van rushed past Wendy's Daihatsu, blue lights throbbing, and entered the intersection recklessly fast, unaware that it had become an accident scene. A gunshot rang out, ripping through the squeal of police sirens. The police van screeched and pulled sideways to avoid smashing into the SUV. It swerved uncontrollably, skidded across the intersection, then smashed sideways into the BMW, pinning Brenda between the two vehicles. The footage that was leaked onto Facebook showed that the van collided with the BMW with such force that it bumped its owner sideways, blonde hair flopping as he sailed through the air and tumbled comically down the hill.

Wendy was frozen once more, eyes locked with Brenda's, the two women staring at one another in disbelief, trapped in a tragic moment that Wendy would carry with her for the rest of her life.

I tried to imagine what pain Brenda must have been in. Looking at the traffic camera footage, not to mention the brutal facts supplied by the responding medics, I was able to deduce that she had been saved from the agony of her injuries. The first paramedic who treated her, a short man with orange hair, said they often encountered patients with stress-induced analgesia, which rendered them momentarily incapable of feeling pain. According to him, Brenda was lucid, not delirious nor panicky, yet she had no pain.

The paramedic and two EMT responders arrived on the scene, poured out of their vehicles with perfected grace, and went about their business with professional urgency. A thin man in a police uniform sat in the rear opening of the police van, an EMT dressing a lesion to one hand. I would later hear from this officer that he had been on the passenger side of the van where my wife had been pinned. He told me that her face had been as white as bone and her hair matted back with perspiration, and when she spoke, it was with noticeable sluggishness. He never told me what she said, though. Whatever it was, it had touched him deeply.

By the time Wendy extracted herself from the safety of her car, baby held close to her chest, the driver of the SUV was seated in the back of one ambulance, and the owner of the BMW had been placed onto a stretcher. She made her way across the intersection with Themba in her arms. The intoxicating and disorienting smell of oil on hot tar caused her to gag, but she had to see. She pushed her way through the small crowd around the BMW. There she saw Brenda on the ground. They had managed to shimmy the BMW aside, thus enabling two EMTs to remove Brenda from where she had been wedged between the two vehicles. Using spider straps, they had secured her to a backboard stretcher before lifting her over the hood of the police van. Wendy explained that her pelvic bone, hips, and legs had been flattened and that there was a lot of blood.

The emergency team moved about, but to no avail. When Brenda noticed Wendy looking down at her, she smiled and then her eyes clouded over. Her smile faded and pulled into a hollowed expression.

I wanted Brenda to have endured pain, for nothing more than the sake of fuelling a rage that was unaccustomed to me. I wanted agony and distress and pain to feed my hatred, but Brenda had decided against it. Even in death, she had deflated my hurt and liberated me from the additional anguish of compunction. That didn't stop me from searching for the culprit, though.

The lead detective later informed me that they had received a tip-off from a pub owner in Rondebosch that morning, after the driver of the blue Golf was spotted collecting drugs from a known location. A surveillance unit tracked the car from Rondebosch up to Durbanville, where they saw the driver dropping loads with street dealers. Police immediately blocked off the main road, hoping to funnel the suspect into a trap. By some fluke, the driver was alerted and sprung the trap early. The police van was the only vehicle able to turn back and give chase.

Following the accident, the traffic cameras showed the driver of the Golf hobbling towards the industrial area, where he disappeared among the factory buildings.

The car's boot contained about two kilograms of cocaine, portioned for distribution to drug runners. The car owner details were no good because the vehicle had been stolen in Namibia a couple of weeks before. The police had nothing to go on. However, in my own search for him, I found something interesting. I came upon a tire fitting centre on the outskirts of the industrial area with a set of cameras overlooking the Old Oak Boulevard intersection, which was the only point of entry from the residential area. With cash on site, their insurance provider agreed to drop their premium if they installed cameras as a deterrent. I sat with the manager and studied the recording for the better part of the day. The footage clearly showed a man limping into Bellville Industrial shortly after the accident.

When I showed the footage to the lead investigator, he pointed out an obscured, yet unmistakably unique tattoo of a dragon's head on the man's right hand. He said the footage would be inadmissible in court, but that he was dead sure the owner of that tattoo was a man named...

CHAPTER 10

"Harold Spickerman," I said to my awaiting audience.

There was a crisp silence. My blood burned like ice in my veins. It was the longest five seconds I had experienced in all my life. It was so silent in the room that I heard a car backfire two blocks away.

"Also known as Harry Spicks," I said, then turned to face my wife's murderer.

Harry Spicks looked down at me with mean, unyielding eyes. His chest heaved and his large hands were balled into fists. He had a trimmed beard, pronounced cheek bones and a short, thick neck. Even in this afternoon heat, he wore a red beanie low over his brow. I could tell that he hadn't anticipated this revelation. He also had no idea how he had affected my life. He did not know me or Brenda. His chief concern was the consequence of the questions about to reign down on him. I imagined he was already preparing answers in his mind. I had expected him to shoot me before dropping his name, but he hadn't. A part of me would have been relieved. It would make no difference if my story was cut short by a bullet. This was just a formality, a delicious ideal for my benefit.

"This is bullshit," he said, then, "Why are you all looking at me?"

Shane carried a sombre look on his face, his forehead was creased. His eyes studied me intensely, peering into me as though he was looking for my soul. He was ruminating over the last part of my story, processing the probability of it.

"When was this? You said this was February." He placed the question in front of me as though that was his play.

"Boss," Harry pleaded.

I nodded.

"You're not buying this, are you?"

Shane's gaze shifted from me to Harry with marked effort. His eyes became cold and brutal. A vicious animal swirled around inside his body, only flesh constricting its true form.

"I remember the accident, but the part about the drugs from Rondebosch is a new development," Shane said.

"The police couldn't release that information because it was an ongoing investigation," I explained.

Another long silence followed.

"Did anyone else know about this?"

Shane's question sent a tangible chill through the room. There seemed to be a general uncertainty about how to respond. Those unfamiliar with Shane's operation cleared their throats, others looked at their shoes, with only a few daring to shake their heads no. Though Denvor remained hidden in the large chair, his sneer radiated from within the depths of the shadows.

"Spicks?" he phrased it as a question, but it was, in fact, an immaculate and terrible judgement that had been deliberated and passed in the hallowed courts of Shane's internal judicial system.

"This guy… He's lying." Harry Spicks waved a hand at me, but it was clear my words had found purchase.

The men to either side of Harry took a quick step away from him, so slight that it almost went unnoticed. Harry sensed the act of abandonment and grew more desperate by the second. His eyes began to panic, flicking about the room as though looking for an exit.

"So," Shane said as his fingers curled around the gun in front of him. "You've been selling Rondebosch smack on the side?"

"Shane," he said softly. He tried a personal plea, but even I could tell his fate had been sealed.

"I guess I'm not paying you enough. What's the price tag on loyalty these days?"

"It's not like that, man."

Shane rose from his chair, almost involuntarily, a whisper of a movement, his lips twisted in anger. "You lied to me," he hissed and raised his weapon. "You are running with another crew."

Denvor also got up. "Not here," he cautioned. "This is a residential area."

"Then you shouldn't have brought this shit to your home. What did you think was going to happen?" Shane fired back without removing his eyes from Harry. His anger did not subside.

Denvor signalled two of his men to intercede and to remove Harry before shots were fired. As the men took hold of Harry, he pulled free and charged at me. He put one large arm around my neck and pulled back until my breath became trapped somewhere in my throat, not coming and not going. I didn't fight it. By this point, I was graciously awaiting the release of death, the black curtain of finality. I closed my eyes and allowed my body to go limp. All resistance fled from me as I yielded. This was it.

My chair was hoisted up, then came down harshly. I heard groans, a string of swear words and then the grip around my throat slackened. Oxygen poured into my lungs as his arm released me and the struggle behind me hushed. I gasped and coughed, like a dog coughing on a bone.

"Who are you?" Harry screamed as they pulled him out the door, his legs flailing and his feet kicking the door back. His voice echoing down the corridor. "Who you working for, man?"

Shane beckoned someone over with a nod. Zahier Moodley, the thin man who did most of Shane's dirty work, readied himself to follow.

"Between the eyes," Shane commanded Zahier. "You hear me? Right between the eyes. Make sure they never find him." Then as an afterthought, "First check the *bra* for wires."

Zahier nodded and left the room. His footfalls followed the scuffling sound of kicking feet. Swear words turned into desperate pleas. Harry's final scream was cut short by a loud, crunching thud that rippled through the house. It was a sickening sound, like that of a bowl banging hard on a marble countertop.

Prior to the day, I had implanted a mental picture of Brenda by meditating on her face, her body, her smile. I had kept it there, fixed in the forefront of my mind, should remorse attempt to hinder my plans. I was concerned that the Harry Spicks matter would derail me, but I had no remorse. I was fully aware of what would happen to Harry, yet I was indifferent. This vexed me still, since over the last couple of months my emotional state had become multifaceted, seldom remaining a certain way for very long. Harry was a cruel monster who prowled the streets in search of lives to devour, but he was still a semblance of life. I wondered whether my plans were solely reserved for the innocents of this drama or whether there was a cancer eating away at my soul.

"You have some nerve, man," Shane said, directing what remained of his confused anger at me. He was scratching his head with the barrel of his gun, which seemed like a curious thing to do.

I had positioned myself upright on the chair once more. My eyes were watering from the strain of a throttled trachea. I coughed a couple times and swallowed a mouthful of frothy spit.

"I'm telling you where the money came from."

"Yeah, you're telling it," Shane repeated in a mocking tone. "You're not telling us shit, *bra*. You only come and upset my business. You think snitching out Spicks wins you graces? That just makes me want to cut your nuts off."

He fell silent and his eyes became distant. There lingered a strange madness within him, an undecided insanity that came and went at will. Lately, I had seen something similar stare back at me in the mirror, though not quite as wild.

"Have you ever cut someone's nuts off? It's not easy getting through that skin. The elasticity… It clings to the blade." His eyes went from distant to present as his sanity returned. He sighed, almost exhausted. "Get to the point, *bra*. Who are you working for? Where's the *nannas*? The money."

I pulled my collar back into place. The thin skin around my neck burned and my throat felt dry. My head was aching again, hiding at the base of my neck, squeezing my eyeballs.

"I need more water," I ventured.

Shane looked at Denvor and laughed hysterically.

"You believe this guy? More water." Then he to me, "You are

funny, Mr. Gray."

"It's just Gray." I said in an annoyed tone. It had taken great effort to create that alias; it felt like home to me.

He feigned an apology and held the gun over his heart as though it formed part of his anatomy.

"Oh, I'm so sorry, Mr. Just Gray. Please, if you will, tell us another story, Mr. Just Gray." He waved his hands about the room. "Please do tell us more."

"Well," I said, eager to use the opportunity before I lost it. "After my wife died, I began plotting how to kill all of you."

This comment removed any evidence of a smile from his features. He stood in the middle of the room, frozen stiff. Swallowed up in thought, he tapped the barrel of the gun against his leg, the tempo of which was congruous to my heart palpitations, blood pulsing so furiously that I felt the rhythmical tickle at the base of my neck.

"All of you," I said, making eye contact with every man in the room.

"Enough," Denvor said. "This is turning into a farce."

"Nah, *bra*, wait," interjected Shane in his notably accentuated slang. "I want to hear this. Someone, go get me some popcorn."

"At your own peril, Shane."

He spun around and glared at Denvor. "My peril? Maybe the boy has something to say about your crew, too?"

"My people are loyal." It came as a decisive blow from Denvor. "I don't need anyone to point out my weaknesses."

"Your people are loyal and mine aren't? Is that how it is, *tjomma*?"

"I told you, I'm not your bloody *tjomma*. This is not a team effort. *You* said he was the guy moving drugs in our area. I'm here because *your* people said he was the new player in town. So far, it sounds more and more like he has beef with you, not me."

Shane sighed, crossed the room, and sat down in his chair just as Zahier re-entered the room. He extended his hand and gently placed the gun on the table without looking up. He stared blankly at the weapon, a playful smile weighing down his pointed chin. I wasn't sure if he was mocking me or seriously engaged. Regardless, there was a lull, and Denvor's annoyance suggested that I was running out of time.

CHAPTER 11

I wish I could remember more about Brenda's funeral. Fellow workers from my office were there, along with people I didn't know. They might have come for the free food and drinks provided by the catering company. After the burial, strangers roamed through my house, my privacy flayed open and everyone peeking at what the innards of normalcy looked like.

The presiding pastor said I was zombie-like in my attendance. He was correct. I navigated my way through proceedings in absentia. It was all so surreal that my cognitive reasoning imploded, or, more accurately, caved in. With every emotional blow, sorrow etched its way further into my being, as though it was seeking that little flame that flickered in the deepest crevices of my soul. When Brenda departed, a toxic puff of wind twirled through the cracks and expunged that flame. My core fragmented and left behind a broken man.

Brenda had played an integral part in overseeing the previous funerals. This realization dealt me a double blow because it led me down the treacherous path where I blamed myself for her death. An error on my part, perhaps, but it didn't stop the idea from sprouting. I fed and nurtured this internal accusation until it destroyed my mind, even more than what it was destroying itself.

Time rolled out in front of me like the endlessness of space. I saw stars and constellations one minute, a distant dark vacuum the next. Existences, those of people entering my sphere of agony, seemed to barge into sight. Yet because I was in such a constant state of flux, they were instantly sucked into a black hole, leaving me with no recollection that they had entered my world. I ended up hurting a lot of people who were sincerely reaching out to me. But my soul was in mourning, which forfeited all accountability.

It was days later that I was finally coaxed out of the house by a beguiling phone call.

The call brought me to the desk of Detective Xhosa. It was cluttered with case files, photos, a weapon cleaning kit, loose bits of stationery and our two Styrofoam cups positioned on opposite sides of the desk, his empty and mine full.

"I apologize for the coffee. This is all we can offer," he said.

I waved the apology aside. Looking at the stale coffee in front of me, I was confused about how it had arrived there. "You asked me to come in, Detective," I said in a low tone. "What is this about?"

Xhosa was standing behind his desk. I was seated in the chair opposite. A part of him looked agitated at the crudeness of my question. Another part of him smelled of pity. There was subtle wisdom in his demeanour, like that of someone who had experienced a great deal in life and seldom reflected on his losses.

I hadn't slept for three days. I didn't care what he thought of me.

"I understand," he said finally, easing himself into the chair.

When I moved, the wooden chair moved beneath me, emitting creaks and cracks. It didn't feel safe to sit in it.

"This must be a difficult time for you."

I nodded, curling my lip.

"Yours is a strange and terrible case. I've never seen things so intertwined before. I'm sorry that life has dealt you this bitter blow of coincidence."

"Coincidence?" I asked.

"Indeed. Profound coincidence."

He finished the remnants of coffee in his cup and repositioned things to make space in front of him. He plonked a file down and opened it to reveal a picture of a lifeless Brenda with both eyes shut.

Xhosa quickly turned the picture over. "Sorry, you were not meant to see that."

"I already saw her like that at the morgue. I had to identify her body."

He stared at me as though he was hoping to instil common sense into me. "Sir," he said softly. "You were not meant to see that again. Once is enough."

The other police officers and detectives I had met with during this part of my life had a less than amicable quality about them. They seemed indifferent, numbed by the reality of their vocation and, consequently, inept at conducting themselves professionally.

Xhosa's gentle manner was slightly out of place in the bustle of the Bellville police station. He had warmth in him which, bizarre as it was at the time, filled me with a sense of hope. This was short-lived, of course. Xhosa was about to ruin my day.

"The coincidence I refer to lies at the root of your present situation. Coincidence ties the death of your brother, to that of your sister-in-law, as well as that of your wife. While your sister-in-law is classified as a suicide and your wife's death is ruled as an accidental death, there is something at the core of it that must be explained to you."

He told me about the link between the shootout wherein Allan had died and the weapon Satí had bought. A forensic ballistics analysis was able to match the bullet that had killed Allan with the bullet that had killed Satí, which meant they had been killed with the same type of bullet fired from the same weapon. The absolute coincidence of Satí purchasing the very weapon that had been used during the restaurant shooting, then shooting herself with the similar type of bullet that had, with a wild and stray trajectory, ended Allan's life, is a statistical anomaly that could rival any odds. After a brief interrogation with the boy who had sold Satí the gun, he brought up the name Malique Dandala. However, Malique was tipped off early into the investigation and fled before they could arrest him. Xhosa explained that Malique was affiliated with Denvor Daniels' entourage. He then added that the Golf which had caused Brenda's death, had been linked to Shane Collins' drug operation. This was before I had been moved to investigate the anonymity of the man behind the Golf's steering wheel. Xhosa said that Daniels and Collins had both been identified at the restaurant shootout. Eyewitnesses changed their statements when the matter progressed, and, as the murder weapon had been recovered in the lifeless hand of the grieving spouse, there was no way to implicate either in Allan's murder.

Once done, he hung his head and offered me a sympathetic smile, which looked like a gentle grimace.

"Our hands are tied in ways that are unfamiliar to us." He waited for a reply. When it didn't come, he added, "I can't even make life difficult for them. Both men have ace legal teams running interference, which keep police at bay." Again, he waited, and again he added, "But we are watching them closely. They will make a mistake."

"So," I said, "Nothing?"

His grimace intensified.

"My brother, my sister-in-law, my mother, and my wife. All gone. And I get no justice? No right for wrong?" I didn't raise my voice. I suspect my coolness terrified Xhosa.

"I am sorry, sir. We…" He stopped himself, rethought his approach. "I will find a way to get justice."

"Clearly, you are unable to do so. You just admitted it."

"Sir…"

I stood up. As I pushed the chair back, the white desk fan tilted over and clattered over Xhosa's desk, pushing files aside and knocking his empty cup off the table. He got up and set the fan upright.

"Detective Xhosa, it is better I sort this out myself. I have loads of time on my hands. *I* will find a way to get justice."

Xhosa held out his hands, looking around as he made a shushing sound.

"Don't say those things here." He motioned me to sit down again. "Please, you mustn't say that. If anyone hears, it can be used against you. The world has become a series of court cases, and the good guys seldom win."

"What am I to do?" I whispered in renewed agitation.

"I understand. I really do. But you can't take them on by yourself. They will kill you and carry on with their business."

"Goodbye, Detective Xhosa."

I strolled through the department in a trance. The long corridor leading to reception had a mesmerizing quality to it, beckoning me towards a tiny square at the end of a dimly lit tunnel while secretly reluctant to expel me from its hold. I signed out at reception and went outside.

The exterior of the building was a red face brick façade with shady lighting and a faded blue SAPD light hidden at the far end. It was almost eight o' clock. The din of daytime pedestrians and the rumble of delivery trucks had passed the torch over to the repetitive hum of Bellville nightlife. The evening air was invigorating and fresh, with a hint of fynbos that wafted down from the Tygerberg Nature Reserve. It carried on the air like pleasant memories. It could be because I had been reclused in my house for some time, depressing my cat and my mother's dog that caused me to readily recall the air.

I was busy making my way out of the gate when I heard it: *Pssst!*

I turned and saw someone's reflection shifting within the shadows. There came another *pssst* sound. Deep within the darkness, a cigarette coal lit up. The orange glow bounced back from Detective Xhosa's cheeks. He was leaning against a wall, out of sight, ensconced in shadow.

Putting apprehension aside, I joined him, more out of curiosity than anything else. I said nothing and kept my hands in my pockets. He began talking, and for some bizarre reason I kept quiet and let him finish.

"It's been almost two years now," he said in a hushed tone. He sucked on his cigarette and expelled the smoke into the shadows. "She was going to get married that weekend. We were having a rehearsal dinner. It was where the turf war was at its fiercest. Between the same two men. She was in a coma for two months, then her body just stopped fighting."

"I'm really sorry to hear that," I said. There was nothing else I could say.

"She was an innocent." He took another draw from the cigarette, then shot the remains of it into the darkness. "Do you see? The innocents are the ones unjustly affected by this."

My unresponsiveness must have expressed my uncertainty about the point he was trying to make. I was not looking for confusion, yet it often found me. On top of that, I've had an insane headache for weeks. It wouldn't yield to painkillers. The pain had intensified until it made my eyes sensitive to light.

"I know of someone," he whispered and stepped into the sombre glow of the streetlights. "Call this guy. Tell him about your innocents." He handed me a piece of paper with a name and a number written on it. "He can help you."

I took the note and stared at it.

"Why didn't *you* call him?"

Detective Xhosa became reflective.

"I did," he said. "But I couldn't go through with it. I had only one cut, one innocent to put to rest. You have many cuts. Call him."

A set of headlights swooped over us as a police van pulled into the drive. I shielded my eyes from the glare as the vehicle rattled past. When I turned back, Detective Xhosa was gone.

I lingered for a moment, pocketed the note and left. I stopped at an all-night pharmacy for stronger pain meds. I've tried paracetamol, aspirin, ibuprofen, and diclofenac to deaden the pain. It was time to try opioids and barbiturates but couldn't get them without a prescription.

The next morning, the doorbell woke me from a disturbing dream. I envisioned slugs crawling along my fingers, leaving slimy trails in their wake. Then I saw them crawling over Brenda's dead face, one slug pulling an eyelid back as it crept over her closed eyes. It repulsed me to think of Brenda in that way. I blamed the person on the other end of the doorbell for this image.

When I opened the door, Bertie September turned around, smiled wanly and pushed his glasses back.

I slammed the door shut before he could say anything.

"Good morning," he said loudly on the other end of the door.

"Piss off!"

"We need to talk about these claims. They are highly unusual."

I left him on the porch and returned to bed.

A couple of days later, I pulled myself together long enough to attempt laundry. I came upon Detective Xhosa's note in my denim pockets. For a further two days, the note lay on the surface of the coffee table where Brenda and I had once made love. When my self-loathing reached a peak and my headache sufficiently fuelled my anger, I picked up the note and called the number. I arranged a meeting at a coffee shop the following morning. I was familiar enough with the layout to know it had nooks where a sensitive conversation could be conducted without worrying about curious ears or prying eyes.

I was 15 minutes early. I sat in the car interrogating myself. I had no idea what fruit the meeting would hold. It was not the type of engagement where lack of possible outcomes made the encounter any more promising. The way I had obtained the note suggested the illicitness of the meeting. I was about to get my hands dirty – and I didn't care. My mental reasoning was in a state of flux. There were no longer clear black or white perspectives, just this large grey battlefield where my thoughts gathered to deliberate, hold caucus, and cast votes, while I stood divided in the black or the white, gawping through the fence as decisions were made in my absence.

The coffee shop was a quaint spot situated between Bellville and Durbanville. The wooden tables and menu designs complemented their use of earthy tones. There were some customers sitting at the display windows overlooking the busy traffic, with a short queue of suited office workers and spandex-clad moms at the counter. Baristas passed barbs at each other, which blended with the beats of the Brazilian lounge fusion music that drifted from speakers overhead, occasionally cut short by the sharp hiss of an espresso machine's steam wand.

I ordered a flat white cappuccino and found a tight spot at the back of the premises. With a high windowsill, the late morning sun leapt over my head and bounced over the corner I had selected, dropping a ball of shadow on the table. We would be trapped in a grey haze for the length of the meeting, with a dividing barrier of light slowly pulling towards me over the adjoining tables, like the sparkling crackle of a lit fuse drawing towards a stick of dynamite.

I was still adjusting to the farting sounds emitting from the edges of the red leather chair, when a short unsuspecting man joined my table as though he was returning from the bathroom.

"Crazy traffic this morning," he said. He studied something on the table menu and made a grumbling sound. He looked questioningly at me. "Well, that's new. Who would eat that?" When the waiter arrived with my coffee, he said, "I'll have the same. Thanks."

As the waiter left, I looked around, naturally suspicious, then leaned closer to my unfamiliar guest.

"Gavin?" I whispered. "Are you Gavin?"

"The one and only," he said loud enough for everyone to hear.

He could tell I was dubious. He sat back and gave me an uncomfortable, dead stare.

"Would people remember someone who acted strange? Or someone who acted like everyone else?"

"Oh, right…" I sat up and leaned into my chair with fake aplomb, at ease for onlookers, yet secretly uneasy in Gavin's presence. "Noted."

"That's better," he said.

A plump waitress with bad acne offloaded his coffee and spun it clockwise until the spoon rattled against the ceramic saucer.

"Mmmm, gorgeous," he said as she waddled off. I wasn't sure if he was talking about the coffee or the waitress.

When she was out of earshot, he asked me where I got his number, though I had already told him over the phone. Either he had forgotten, or he was making sure my source hadn't changed since the day before. I told him again.

"The fact that I get most of my business from police officers should tell you a lot."

"A lot about what?"

"About the state of our country. About our police services."

I nodded thoughtfully and wondered if he had a military background.

His eyes were all over the show, as if he was watching the metal ball in a pinball machine ricochet off flippers and bumpers. He was a short man with broad shoulders. He wore a khaki jacket with an upended collar and a small cap, which obscured his features. His short stubby fingers were busy when they were in sight, arguing amongst themselves or fiddling with sugar packets.

"Alright, so what do you need?" he asked.

I told him my tale of woe, adding the information from Detective Xhosa, stressing the police's inability to ensure the course of justice.

"Justice?" Gavin scoffed. "What a strange word. Almost the same as truth."

"You don't believe in justice?"

"I believe in wrath."

"Does that mean you right wrongs?"

"Ah…" His menacing smile suspended between his bunched-up cheeks. "But what seems right to you, might be wrong to the recipient of your wrath."

I waited for a young couple to pass our table, smiling involuntarily.

"So, you would just as easily right me if I was the other person's wrong?" He didn't answer. I carefully considered his non-response, then rephrased the question. "Do you work for any of the men I mentioned?"

"I'm meeting with you first, which makes *you* my client." He downed the rest of his drink and pushed the empty cup to one side.

"Detective Xhosa said you could help me in my quest for justice."

I thought that remark would annoy Gavin, but it didn't. His eyes flickered, fingers fumbled, face tightened. His smile became criminal, revealing his teeth in a similar way a determined Dobermann once bared its teeth at me. He leaned closer to ensure that no one could hear him.

"You want these men to disappear, yes?"

I nodded.

"Will that right the wrong?" he asked as though he was addressing a naughty child.

I nodded.

"Great," he said. "Justice will cost you fifty thousand per head. That's a hundred grand for both. Cash up front." He slid a small SIM card across the table. "I'll call you on this number tomorrow and arrange a drop."

"Fifty thousand up front," I said, almost surprised to hear myself negotiate terms with a hitman. "Fifty upon completion."

Gavin stared at me for a long time, his eyes narrowing slowly until he glared at me through slits. He smiled suddenly and got up.

"I'll call you tomorrow," he whispered and left as the sun crept over the edge of the table.

I expelled a troubled sigh and dropped down on my elbows, hoping that it would stop my world from turning. It didn't. I pondered about what I'd just done. I had set in motion a contract to have two men murdered. And I was unfazed by it. I was more concerned with my headache. My head throbbed and buzzed. It felt like a strange throwback to my clubbing days and how the strobe lights flashed along with the thump of the techno beats. There was a similar thumping sound in my ears one moment and an incessant pinging sound the next. At times, it was excruciating.

When I returned to the car, I pinched the bridge of my nose until my eyes began to water. I put the seat back and tried resting my eyes, but nothing helped. I called my doctor and made an appointment for the following day. I needed stronger medication, but no amount of coaxing could convince a pharmacist to relinquish control of the good stuff they kept hidden behind the counter. I have exhausted all conventional over-the-counter options.

From the coffee shop, I drove around town and stopped at different ATMs. I withdrew most of the required funds from my personal account and the rest from Brenda's savings account which was still active. I had spousal signing authority, so I reasoned that I was emptying her account with the intention of closing it at a later stage. Even from a distant astral plane, Brenda's absent disapproval weighed heavy on my soul.

I went home, put the fifty thousand Rand in a large envelope and hid it under my office desk. After that I took a handful of painkillers and flipped through channels until my eyelids became like lead-filled curtains. Eventually everything went black. There, lost in the dark memories where my make-believe past and my forever-after future converged, I bowed down to the will of my nightmares, tormented until daylight called me back to the land of   the   living.

CHAPTER 12

The empty sockets of an anatomical model studied me from the edge of the desk. Its smooth skull was slanted, askew from the rest of its fleshless skeletal structure, bony feet dangling at awkward angles. It was pivoted in such a way that it peered down at me with an air of judgement, its jaws agape and its hands partially extended, as though it was giving pursuit.

As the clouds played around outside, obscure shadows inflated and deflated against the soft cream-colored vertical blinds. At times, the room grew dark enough for the fluorescent bulbs to have their desired effect. When the clouds filtered away, the room became blindingly white, which felt like piercing shards of glass pressing into my eyeballs.

It took me a while to remember where I was or how I had gotten there. This incessant headache was causing my memories to play hide-and-seek. For most of that morning, I had forgotten about the hitman I had under my employ. When it hit me, I panicked, until the headache returned. Then I became stolid once more. I didn't trust myself. My reasoning seemed off. Which brought me back to the skeleton on the desk.

Doctor Immelman stopped writing for a few seconds. He raised his bushy brows and closed his eyes, evidently vexed by my headaches. He found the word he was searching for and continued writing. The sound of his pen scraping across the texture of the paper was deafening in the tense silence.

He was about sixty, balding, pudgy-faced and short. In the ten years I'd known him, I found him to be precise, efficient and painfully direct. Brenda had thought the world of him, which was enough of a conviction for me.

"Righty-oh," he said in a peculiar, high-pitched voice. "I see you've tried a lot of different drugs here. And it's been, what, about eight weeks?"

I looked at him through narrow eyelids and shook my head. "I honestly can't remember. I think it's been long enough to be concerned."

"Dear boy," he said softly and leaned forward on his elbows. "You should have been concerned in that first week. The sound in your ears is very alarming."

"I know, but it's been a crazy time. There wasn't really…"

"I understand. I really do. And it's OK. You are here now." He closed the file and sat back. "So, I can give you something that would take the pain away post-haste, but it might just come back again. Or we can investigate the problem by doing a flyover in the opposite direction and at a higher altitude. Like the aeronautical manoeuvre." My vacant stare peeled the smile off his face. "Let's find out what's really going on in there."

"I can't deal with this pain anymore. Can you at least stop the pain while we investigate?"

"I certainly can. I'm sure it's nothing, but let's not rule anything out. Normally I wouldn't be too drastic, but you've had it rough. The body doesn't respond well to the type of stress you've endured." He gave me a sympathetic nod, pursed his lips, then pulled his notepad closer and began writing again. "I suggest we do an initial scan first and if that's clear, we can follow up with blood tests. This will help us narrow it down. Your medical aid should cover it. Does your plan have any exclusions?"

"I haven't a clue. If I must pay, I'll pay."

"I'm also prescribing something with a bit more *oomph*. Be sure to take it after you are at home or in a safe environment." He slid a prescription note across his desk and offered me a playful smile. "And don't operate heavy machinery after taking those."

He also gave me a reference letter with his illegible scribbles on and sent me to the radiologist two floors up. I went up by elevator to make a booking, humming a tune to myself as the cables pulled the metal box into position. The radiologist had an opening, so I walked straight into a breezy blue hospital gown. I sat waiting for a while, feeling dejected and on display, then I was ushered into the room where the scans were conducted. A young, attractive nurse with long eyelashes and symmetrical hips asked some questions and I answered. She steered me back until the patient table pressed against my backside. When I turned, my breath caught in my chest. A ripple of reality washed over me when I saw the massive tube-shaped dome of the magnet housing looming in front of me.

Soon enough the scan was done. It was still early, so I headed home and took my new meds. I began unpacking Brenda's clothes; a task I loathed. I'd purposely delayed it, but every time I opened her cupboards, a dagger of remorse pierced through my spirit and pinned me to the couch in a distressing state, TV remote glued to my hand. The big clean-out had to be done, for my own sanity. I was hoping that once Brenda was out of sight, she would be out of mind. It's not that I wanted to forget her. I just couldn't cope anymore. My life was falling apart faster than I could put it back together. I had no purpose, nothing worth fighting for.

The bed was stacked with her shirts, dresses, sandals, boots, slip-ons, running shoes, scarves, cardigans, panties, bras, socks, belts, handbags, make-up, and her wedding dress, which she had kept as a memento in case we adopted a daughter one day. I put her jewellery into a small box. There weren't many, but since I had bought most of it, every piece had a sentimental connection that rested in my mind like tiny burdens that grew in size whenever I looked at them. Compiling all her things was a meek attempt at ridding the house of the memories we had shared. Then there was the dirty cup with a smudge of her lipstick curled around the edge, the smell of her perfume that lingered in every corner of the house, the odd strain of her hair stuck on my clothes, Moscow's utter disappointment when I arrived home with no Brenda in tow, the endless supply of photos, all her old voice notes that I frequented every night before stealing away to the misery that waited for me in our bedroom. It was just getting too much. My mind was carving out hollow pockets of resentment towards my former happiness.

I was busy putting everything into black bags when Brenda's phone began to vibrate, rattling across the top of her dressing table. I stared at the phone in alarm. It took me a while to remember that I had put the hitman's SIM card into Brenda's old phone. The reflection of my face in the dressing table's mirror gave me chills. I almost didn't recognize myself with a beard.

Facial hair never really suited me, but a neglected beard on my cheeks looked woeful. My eyes looked unfamiliar to me, almost creepy. As internal changes were taking effect and shooting out roots, external changes were starting to show.

I answered the phone but didn't utter a word. I was greeted by an uncomfortable silence, then Gavin's menacing voice reached through the phone and crept into my ears.

"Thirty minutes. Same place. Bring the package."

The phone went dead.

I finished bagging Brenda's clothes, using the cold act of doing so to motivate my intentions. Every garment had blood on it. She had been an innocent. Her blood was scattered over every memory that I held onto. As my eyes hardened in the reflection of the mirror, I realized that an unknown part of me wanted blood for blood, even if it came at the hands of a hitman whom I completely distrusted.

Money in hand, I left the house. I arrived five minutes late and found Gavin sitting with his back to the wall, which was the same seat I had previously chosen. The tables had turned. When I sat down, it was as though I was sitting down with the devil. Gavin's demeanour was different. He was colder somehow. His face carried a wrinkled forehead, furrowed brows, and tight lips. His eyes were no longer playful. It felt as though he was considering me, studying me, looking for a way to snake into my being and devour my soul. I wondered whether he had a split personality that orchestrated the dirty part of his job, like a different puppet master pulling the strings.

"You're late," he hissed.

"Five minutes," I said. "Is that a problem?"

"Don't ever come late again or I'll kill you."

An ice wave swooped over my body. The area around our table became blisteringly hot and wintry cold at the same time. Time froze. The suddenness and nonchalance of his threat left me without words or thoughts. My lips were pressed together so tightly that it began to hurt at the edges where it closed over my teeth. Somewhere inside my mind I was at war with myself, but when something rattled me, the two parts became one and clarity returned.

"Did you bring it?"

I blinked a couple of times, as though I was flipping through pages of a book to catch up to the story. I pushed the envelope across the table.

"It's all there," I muttered, my mouth suddenly dry.

"Of course, it is." A grim smile spread across his face as he pocketed the package. "You are too clever to renegotiate." He was about to leave, but I stopped him.

"I have a request, please."

"You have exhausted your requests."

"This is different." He eased back and waited, momentarily stalled by the vice of curiosity. "I want to see," I said, more surprised about the words dripping from my lips than Gavin. I had no control over my thoughts. "I *need* to see it."

He leaned into the seat and studied me carefully, putting my soul under scrutiny once more. "I never took you for the type. I thought I had you pegged, but there's something off in you, like spoilt meat. Yeah, I see it now."

"What do you mean?"

"Does death excite you?"

The idea of death repulsed me. "Not at all. But this is personal. I need to see you do it."

"I'll sleep on it," he said after a while.

Gavin slid out from the booth and rose to his feet. As he looked down at me, a long shadow pulled across his features. His deep-set eyes suddenly resembled the empty sockets of the anatomical skeleton in Doctor Immelman's office.

"You have no idea what you just got yourself into, do you?"

I didn't know how to reply, so I shrugged. Gavin left.

I didn't think it wise to linger, so I went to my office to clear out my desk and to meet a colleague. After Brenda's death, I had resigned. My clients understood. How could they not? I handed them over to a financial adviser I trusted; a slender, hollow-cheeked man called Bob Sampson. I even signed a document that empowered him to tend to my own matters. I did not want to think about the truckload of money heading my way and then still contemplate what to do with it. I gave that task to Bob. He examined the totality of my portfolio, then double-lined an amount on a notepad. While some payments were still in transit, it was just an estimate, though a fairly accurate one. Bob studied the laptop screen, looked sideways at the amount he had jotted down, then whistled softly.

He had two potted plants in his office. A fern that was fighting to stay alive and a miniature aloe with spikes around each succulent leaf blade. They were at war with the mundanity of a financial advisor's office. Soon they would relent, and Bob would replace them with newer, greener alternatives.

"That can't be correct," he whispered and rechecked his figures, a long finger tapping the pointy part of his chin. Satisfied that it was correct, he looked at me over his spectacles. "You are looking at about forty million, give or take."

The amount didn't register at first. The words reached me, but the notion of money held no value to me. It was the most peculiar thing. I had R40 million to spend, but the thought of spending it eluded me. What was the point of having it if I couldn't enjoy it with Brenda. The sum of it all seemed like bribe money, stained with loss.

"Forty…" I mumbled, lost in a trance.

I studied the little aloe and its sharp thorns. The muted daylight that poured in through the office window caused the aloe to become translucent. I could make out the individual cells in each blade and the gel inside the plant's leaf. I found it bizarre how threatening those thorns looked the one instant, and how fragile the tiny thing looked the next. For the first time in my life, sitting there in Bob's office, numbers had no meaning to me.

"Forty," Bob repeated, his bony cheeks betraying his frown. He studied the Eiffel Tower-shaped wall clock, hinting that he had another client scheduled soon. "If you work carefully with this money, you can go see the world and never have to work again. What are your plans?"

The weight of all that money baring down on me, settled over my neck like a heavy yoke meant for two animals. Only I had no partner to share the burden of spending all that money. I was a lone ox pulling a cart overloaded with fortune and weighed down by good intentions.

"I have no idea."

"I'm preaching to the choir here, but you know what we advise clients who feel the way you do now. Put it in a safe investment until you know what to do."

In my troubled state, I decided to do the exact opposite. "I want you to invest it in the most volatile investment you can find."

"Excuse me?" He sat back in alarm, flabbergasted. His skin almost turned white in mere seconds. He removed his glasses and rubbed his temples, a methodical gesture done by financial advisers to feign sympathy. "Listen, you need to be clever about this. I know you had a difficult time, but this is crazy. Trials come and go. You still have your health. You are still young enough to have a semblance of a life. Just ..." He stopped himself short, re-evaluated his words, "Just think about what you are doing."

"Bob, I appreciate your words, but you speak of things you do not understand. Things I don't even understand. While I'm full of confusion about the hand I've been dealt, I'm of sound mind and I'm totally aware of the risks I'm taking. So please allocate the funds as instructed."

His shoulders sagged. It was my money. I was the client. He was the adviser. I had been in that seat before. There was no changing the mind of a resolute investor at the end of his rope.

"Sure thing," he said. "As you wish. How risky do you want to go?"

"All the way. The riskiest investment you can find. I don't care. Send me the proposals and we can take it from there."

I signed the required documents, got up to leave, then stopped at the door.

"There was an annoying claims investigator who came to see me," I said.

"What for?"

I shrugged. "He made it clear he was suspicious about the nature of all the claims."

"Suspicious of what?"

I gave another shrug.

"Sounds a bit weird but let me check into it. I wouldn't worry, though. As unique as your matter is, there is nothing underhanded going on." Bob jotted down a reminder to ask around. "Then again, claims investigators also have a job to do, and insurance companies are always looking for a way out of settlement. Your multiple claims probably set off some red flags."

On my way home, Doctor Immelman's assistant called. She asked if I could come in to discuss the results of my scans. I was close to Brackenfell, so I went straight to his office. It was late afternoon when I stopped outside the building. An ambulance raced in the opposite direction as I got out, then pulled up to the hospital entranceway across the road. A nurse and an EMT went about offloading a patient on a stretcher, then wheeled the patient into the ER entrance.

The clouds that threatened to blot out the sun earlier had succeeded in doing so. Teams of dark puffs spread across the skyline, now seemingly without end. They had amassed so gradually that I hadn't noticed the cold air taking hold of my arms. As I rubbed my arms, I realized I hadn't eaten all day. More alarming was the fact that I wasn't hungry. My appetite had been erratic the last couple of weeks, and it was worsening by the day.

"Same-day service," I joked as Doctor Immelman entered the room. "You give the government a run for its money."

He didn't smile. His face looked grave and tense.

"We were lucky the radiologist had a gap when you were here," he said as he spread the scans and the accompanying disc across his desk. He held one of the images up to the fluorescent lights and slowly shook his head.

"I don't understand."

"Righty-oh," he said, more to the skeleton man on his desk

than to me. He jumbled the scans together as though they were sensitive legal documents, then intertwined his thick fingers. He sighed and looked intently at me. His delayed response and the depth of his stare suggested that he was grappling with something. "We discussed your scans at length. They show an area that is a bit of a concern. It looks like a black spot near the frontal cortex. I'm not a neurologist, but as luck would have it, my brother is. So, as a precaution, I sent the images to him for an expert opinion."

I waited, but he just sat there rubbing his fingers together, his deep blue eyes wavering, evaluating various approaches.

"What?"

"It doesn't look good, I'm afraid. The MRI shows what might be a tumour inside your brain."

I repaid his curtness with a little giggle, but his glare expressed the seriousness of the report.

"Oh, come on. You can't be serious. This must be a joke. I don't understand…" The doctor gave me a moment to digest the information. "Are you saying I have cancer?"

"Nothing's set in stone yet, but we need to get clarity on these scans right away."

"No. This can't be right. It just can't. I mean…"

The sensation of perspiration spreading across my forehead made me panicky. It tickled and crawled across my scalp as my concerns hastened the onset of the perspiration. Deep inside my mind a door was closing, the long blade of light narrowing and fading as it pulled back into its frame.

"I understand your surprise. I took the liberty of explaining your situation to my brother. What you have been through… For the sake of clarity, he has agreed to see you right away."

"Doctor, I don't understand what's happening."

I'm pretty sure I started heaving at this point, though I won't be able to commit to that description. A sudden spell of nausea hit me in my gut. My head spun furiously. It was as though the office was turning over on itself. The more I tried to get air into my lungs the more inadequate it seemed. I rested my head in my hands and pulled in a deep breath. When I closed my eyes, my stomach pushed back against the diaphragm muscles working to create space for my lungs. I focused on a tiny cut in the blue industrial carpeting to stop the room from spinning around. From that point on things became involuntary.

Experiencing a bout of claustrophobia, I jumped to my feet. I went for the door. It was a tragic attempt to escape the confinement. I never made it, though. The door handle approached, fast, coming right at me, a large and shiny object. Then there was a bright flash, which coincided with the sensation of being shook violently. A bank of black clouds pressed in on me from all angles and sucked me into an abyss.

CHAPTER 13

When I came to, I was in a hospital bed. I could tell it was a hospital before I even opened my eyes. The coarse linen pulled across my skin as I wrestled my arms free from its grip.

My eyelids were heavy. My mouth was dry, my jaws were tired, and my tongue was sensitive where I had bitten into it. There was a grating sound in my ears every time I blinked. I could smell I hadn't brushed my teeth in a while. When I wrinkled my forehead, a sharp pain shot through my entire face. Though physically exhausted, I felt wired, as though I had imbibed way too much coffee. I raised one hand, but my fingers shook so violently that I had to relent. As memories refreshed themselves, I realized I must have passed out in the doctor's office and hit my head on the door's handle.

"Ah, good," a voice said beside me. "You are awake."

A man in his early fifties was making notes on a clipboard. His hair was a wavy brown-grey mash-up. He had a comforting smile and a set of eyes that felt familiar, almost calming.

"I'm Dr. Immelman." He smiled. "The other Immelman. You can call me Andre." I saw no resemblance.

I scanned the room. Stark whites and neutral blues. There was a blank television screen mounted to the ceiling above my bed, a chair occupied by a see-through bag containing my clothes, a door leading off to a toilet and a privacy curtain pulled halfway across one side of my bed. The air conditioning system hummed pleasantly in the background.

"Where am I?"

"The hospital across from my brother's practice," he said. "How are you feeling?"

"A bit…" My thoughts collapsed. "Woozy, but not really woozy. Like I've been exercising too long." I tried to sit up, but I was exhausted. "What happened?"

"You had a nervous breakdown," Andre said with a tense smile. "Your system shut down long enough for you to recalibrate, like a laptop rebooting itself."

"Why?"

Andre Immelman drew up the chair, put the bag of clothes on my bedside drawer, and sat down. He closed the pages on the clipboard and lay it down near my feet.

"Severe emotional distress. I suspect you were not sleeping well, either. And bingeing on pain meds. You needed rest and your nerves needed to recalibrate, so your body interceded. You've been asleep for two days."

"Two days? That can't be. I was just in the doctor's office."

"I know it must be disorienting. We kept you on intravenous feeding and, based on the MRI my brother requested, we allowed you to sleep. While you were out, we acquired approval from your medical aid and conducted further scans."

I felt the bump on my forehead. It wasn't as swollen as I'd thought. The bruise tingled as my fingers sailed over the skin. I cringed, then coughed dryly, attempting to clear my throat.

Andre helped me to sit up, then handed me a glass half-filled with water.

"Two days?" I asked again. "It seems surreal."

"Yup, you slept through it all. We didn't even have to sedate you."

I finished the water, cleared my throat, then handed the glass back. Andre waited patiently for me to catch up. He sat cross-legged, one hand propped under his chin and the other's long fingers playing with a pen.

"Scans? What scans?" I asked.

"All of them."

"And?"

"We were able to surmise that you have advanced glioblastoma."

"Glio… What?"

"Brain cancer," Andre said softly. "You have advanced brain cancer."

I swallowed a mouthful of clay as my throat tightened up.

"How advanced?"

"Very. Stage 4."

"What does that mean?"

"It means the tumour you have inside your head is not only aggressive, but it has metastasized to other parts of your brain, which makes it inoperable." He uncrossed his legs and sat forward, elbows on his knees, fingers intertwined in a similar manner to that of his brother. "And fatal."

"Fatal?"

Andre nodded. His lips were pursed.

"How long do I have?"

"It's almost impossible to say. We are unable to gauge how long it took to get to where it is currently. We have no frame of reference here. It could be weeks. It could be months."

A defensive attitude flared up inside of me. My breathing became strained.

"Not years?"

Without removing his eyes, Andre shook his head no. "Statistically, that's unlikely."

The rest of the conversation was a blur. My mind got stuck in the mud midway. I imagined battling to pull my cart laden with riches, then saw the cart's wheels dig deeper into the mud when I added another ten million Rands from a dreaded disease claim against my life policy. I was no longer in control.

Having eaten my hospital lunch, I checked out of the hospital later that afternoon. I asked the hospital staff to assist with submitting my life policy claim to my insurance provider. I signed the necessary documents at reception and left. As the sliding doors in the entranceway parted, something stirred inside of me. It was as though my own personal map was being unfurled on a large table, revealing my most intimate places and my most private thoughts. I was the jungle and the adventurer at the same time. I saw unexplored valleys and peaks within myself that I had never imagined were there, etched into the fabric of my soul map. This stimulus for introspection had been roused by the doctor's bad news, but I couldn't come to terms with my own looming mortality in a hospital bed. I believe, more than anything, I desired to return home. Though the house reminded me of Brenda, it was still my only refuge. It was the one place where I could enjoy unquestionable solitude, which was exactly what I needed after the day's revelations. I had arranged to meet with

Doctor Andre Immelman about my diagnosis and the way forward, if, indeed, there were to be a way forward.

My car was in the parking lot where I had left it two days before. I could tell by the shine on the car that someone had washed my car after the previous day's rains. A nurse had informed me about the sudden arrival of hail and lightning, and how they had made bets to see if the thunderclaps would summon me from my slumber. She said I had cost her R30 in my absence. I apologized.

It was a sunny day, but there was evidence of the deluge. The pavement's darkened tar, clumps of debris caking the sewer grates, and the smell of steam.

I slipped the parking attendant a R100 for washing my car. His joy was unequalled, much like my dismay. As I made my way to my car, I wondered about his life and what the total sum of his joy would be. Was he married? Did he have children? His lack suddenly seemed idyllic when compared to my abundance. I got into my car and headed home.

The comforting warmth of my house had been replaced by the dank smell of rot. At first, I thought it was the banana peels I had left in the trash. Maggots were crawling out of the dustbin in hordes, like an army of motivated soldiers driven to overthrow their opponent. Though tiny, they made a sickening crunch as I stepped over them to get to the broom closet. However, as I reached the broom closet, I discovered the true origin of the stench.

Moscow and Sheba were sprawled out over the kitchen floor, their tummies swollen in death. It appeared that, overtaken by intense hunger, Sheba had pawed open the kitchen sink cabinet and rummaged through the ingredients on the lazy Susan. There the duo must have found Moscow's secret catnip treats. Motivated by their discovery, or high on nepetalactones, they continued ransacking the cabinet and devoured most of the rat poison and snail bait, which must have smelled like tasty snacks. The irony was that the dry foods and edible long-life products were stored in the cabinet opposite the sink base cabinet. Sheba's old nose had led her to the wrong storage space.

The local veterinary doctor later explained that the rate of consumption and amounts ingested would have resulted in a near-instantaneous death for both. The fact that the animals didn't suffer long did little to curb my suffering. Sheba had been the last remembrance of my mother, while Moscow had been the muted echo of Brenda that still lingered in the house. While I was receiving the diagnosis of my terminal illness, both these treasured memories had been dealt a fatal blow. Why I hadn't left a window open or at least put food out for them was beyond my understanding.

Death had made itself welcome in my life and it was refusing to leave. It was ever-present in every nook. Wherever I went and whatever I did, death followed and pushed the glimmer of life further out of my reach. I wanted to scream at the world, tear my clothes and pull out what little hair I had left, but the thought of launching into an exhaustive diatribe and flinging it into the mysterious depths of the heavens above seemed futile.

Later, I went outside and began destroying my backyard. I inspected the hole I had dug. I couldn't remember digging the hole, yet there it was. It was a pathetic-looking mess of a hole. One meter deep, ragged along the sides and terribly dark. My arms, legs, and part of my shirt were dusted with dark earth. Sweat was dripping from my brows. My breathing was strained, partly because I was on the verge of having another panic attack. I had this urge to cry but nothing came of it. I only managed this dry heaving sound accompanied by a soft moan. It was as though my body had no will to lament, yet I was open to embracing the direness of my situation.

I had chosen a spot in the bedding where Brenda had planted an ice cream bush a couple of years before. The shrub's green, cream, and pink leaves were so pleasant to look at. Brenda had loved this plant more than any other. It had been her garden showpiece when visitors came to visit, her pride and joy. I hadn't been able to appreciate its beauty quite as I did at that moment. As I laboured for breath, I stood mesmerized by its obscurity. Though neutral and cold, almost indifferent, the bush was alight with a natural kind of glow that bounced off its leaves and hung in the midday heat like a swarm of gnats.

"Oh my…" an irksome voice said behind me.

Bertie September's curious eyes looked hungrily at me from the other side of the garden gate. Because he was short, I imagined he had to stand on tiptoe to see over the gate. And what a sight it must have been of me wielding the flat blade of a spade, knee-deep in a shallow grave. The towel-covered parcel next to me would have been enough for anyone to be instinctively wary. The insurance claims investigator, however, thought it appropriate to slip the galvanized latch back, push the gate until its hinges squeaked, and proceed to enter my backyard. He stepped awkwardly across the lawn until he was close enough for me to whack him over the head with the spade. I didn't, but the thought of doing it was at the forefront of my mind.

"Well, well, well," he said. "What do we have here? Destroying evidence, are we?"

I clambered out with great effort and positioned myself on the opposite side of the hole, adjusting my grip on the spade, unaware that my knuckles had tightened around the handle.

"You have entered my property without my permission, Mr. September. I am within my rights to defend myself against an intruder."

Bertie seemed unfazed by my remark. His beady eyes hopped over the scene.

"Wouldn't that be something?" he squeaked in a pitched, whiny voice. "Murder in self-defence? Besides, I wouldn't fit into that hole."

"You would fit if your limbs were separated from your torso." The words came without restraint. It was unlike me to be so cruel, but I had no control over my tongue. "What are you doing here? What do you want from me?"

He licked his lips in a manner that seemed to be goading me. I suspect he longed for me to do something that would prove his initial assessment of me. I couldn't fathom what about my situation had convinced him that there was something clandestine at work. At that point, I just couldn't care. I was coming to terms with the fact that I was a dying man. Bertie's view of me held no sway over my future.

"I want to catch you. I want to know how you did it. And why. And then I want you to confess your sins. That will just be better for everyone."

I bent over and pulled the towel back to reveal the two deceased pets. Bertie jumped back in surprise; his excitement was momentarily replaced by repulsion. He shielded himself and held a hand to his mouth, as though he was about to vomit. Then, as I saw his dark mind turning things over, his shock subsided and was replaced by intrigue. A sick joy unfolded in his shiny eyes. He bit his bottom lip and wiped his sweaty palms against his pants as a child might when it gets excited.

"Yes!" he shouted. "Of course. Pet insurance. You slick bastard."

Indeed, both animals had been insured. An insurance company would pay out R10,000 each if both pets passed away. Around the time that Moscow came into our lives, my company was trialling a new custom-made insurance cover product that catered to pet owners. Since we didn't have kids, insurance seemed like a good idea. After my mother passed away, we added Sheba to the policy.

"They died while I was in hospital, you prick."

"Of course," he hissed. He studied me with absolute uncertainty, looking for lies. "What are you hiding? There must be something. Things like this do not simply happen to someone for no reason. You caused this somehow."

I got down to my knees and gingerly picked up Sheba. Her head fell to one side, eyes shut, mouth open. I leaned over and lowered her body into the hole. Her body thumped as it struck the bottom of the grave. Then I slid my hands underneath Moscow's legs and carefully raised his body up. Inside my mind, I pictured Moscow as a kitten, crawling around Brenda's arms, playing with her fingers, biting the drooping curls of her hair. I remembered Moscow's warm body between us on the bed, his deep purr. Brenda's happiness had been like a drug to me. Moscow had been the instrument that fed that happiness. Laying him to rest only reminded me of the burden of having lost my life partner.

I reluctantly let go of Moscow. The cat landed on top of

Sheba's body and curled over, its neck twisting back as though it was judging me from the bottom of the shallow grave.

At that point, my heart caved in. Tears flowed down my cheeks. I had never experienced anything similar. It dawned on me that there was no one who needed my strength, my input, or my support, and no one who could offer me the same in return. I had no purpose. Everything was meaningless, like dust carried off in the wind. There, hunched over in a heap in my backyard, I felt my soul fracture.

Bertie September was so alarmed by my sorrow that he turned and ran out the backyard, the gate latch slapping into place in his wake. I heard his little Honda blare to life and speed off.

I don't know how long this bout of sadness lasted, but it felt like an eternity. I was exhausted. I had nothing more to offer the grave. My hands were tender when they gripped the handle of the spade again. I was a numbers guy, not a gardener, nor a fighter. Thirty minutes of swinging a gardening tool had created blisters inside both palms.

I filled the hole as the sun died away in the field behind my house. Afterward I collapsed on the couch, smearing dark earth everywhere. I clutched the blanket that had last been over Brenda's bare legs, soiling it with my dirty hands. I left the side door open to hear the crickets and the frogs as I drifted into a deep   sleep.

CHAPTER 14

Brenda's phone woke me up late the next morning. Gavin sounded amused by the exhaustion evident in my gruff voice. He hinted at a late night of debauchery, then gave me an address and a time. He reminded me not to be late. He hung up before I could reply.

I was starving. I was weak from not having eaten the day before. There were not enough time or ingredients to prepare something at home. I had to meet Gavin in three hours at a factory building, so I decided to catch breakfast on the way.

Brenda's full-length mirror had been shattered by a wandering fist. Large slivers remained in the frame, with some shards scattered on the floor. I couldn't remember breaking it, but the cuts on my hand and the bruises on my knuckles convicted me of the act. My reflection bounced back and forth off the bits of metal amalgam as I shifted from one foot to the other. I was a shocking sight. My hands and feet were earth-darkened, my clothes grimy and my eyes sunken. It looked as though I'd clawed my way out of a grave, determined to avenge my own death.

In the shower, I scrubbed at the dried dirt under and around my nails to remove any trace of my stint as a gravedigger. I was mesmerized by the soap foam, which twirled around the shower trap grid until it gurgled down the drain. It was a cathartic experience, so visceral that it required intense appreciation. After a quick shave, I was ready for the day.

I had a three-cheese omelette and two cappuccinos at a small coffee shop before setting off to meet Gavin. It was a Sunday morning, as good a morning as any other to watch an assassination. The roads were deserted. Traffic wasn't bottlenecking as it would on a weekday morning. At one stage, I passed a church. The sound of people singing hymns was oddly comforting – yet also distressing. I was not there to do God's work. I was there for malice, to exact revenge. The fact that I was paying someone to do it on my behalf, notwithstanding. I guess a part of me rebelled against the idea of letting a hitman do my dirty work, but my mind and my soul were divided.

I made it to the old glass factory ahead of schedule to avoid another verbal lambasting from my hitman. I took the route around the back of the property as instructed. I pulled up to the large gate I was told to look out for. The red and black obscenity spray-painted across the metal sheeting was impossible to miss. It had been rusted through near the outer extremes where early morning dew had caused the iron oxide residue to leave orange tear tracks, as though the gate was crying rust.

I was about to get out of my car when the gate rippled and shuddered. A small opening appeared, with Gavin's careful eyes peering out at me from beyond. The gate glided inward, leaving a narrow space for me to drive through. Once through, my rear-view mirror revealed Gavin closing the gate with lock and chain.

My little Toyota bumbled across the yard, hitting every

possible pothole in sight. Gavin pointed out a secluded spot at the edge of the property. My car disappeared into the overgrown shrubbery and wild grass. The yard we were in was adjacent to the factory. It was a vacant lot, though it was cluttered with all manner of building debris and large stacks of rotten wood pallets.

When I climbed out, Gavin was on top of me. He took hold of my one arm, swirled it around and had me pinned to the Toyota's bonnet before I could catch my breath. Within seconds he searched my pockets and my body. Not finding a listening device or a weapon, he let go my arm.

"What the hell are you doing here?" he demanded.

I flung around and glared at him. He wore a brown beanie, khaki jacket, cargo pants, brown boots and tight-fitting gloves. His chest heaved and his face was bunched up in annoyance.

"You told me to meet you here."

"I didn't think you were dumb enough to come."

"What do you mean?"

He shook his head, an eerie smile creeping across his face.

"You are crazy, you know that?" He turned and crossed the yard, hunched over. "Come with me."

I followed. The long weeds and grass brushed against my face, obscuring my view and smacking into my mouth. I sneezed involuntarily, which caused Gavin to shoot a displeased look at me.

"Where'd you park your car?" I asked as we pushed further into the weeds.

He stopped and looked at me for a long time. "Why?"

I shrugged. "Just wondering how you got here."

"That's not important. What's important is that I'm here. Now shut up and stay behind me."

We reached a dividing fence that had been broken open in a couple of places. Gavin moved towards a Judas gate inside the larger fence and pushed through it. I steadied myself against the open Judas gate, the rotten wood felt soft in my hand, like an old sponge or a living thing. For the sake of not leaving physical evidence at a crime scene, I made a mental note not to touch anything else. I dipped my head low, stepped over the broken edge of the Judas gate and pushed through after Gavin.

The old glass factory building rose into the skies in front of us. I had read about the factory in the local newspapers. The business had undergone liquidation a while ago and was never able to reopen. One of my clients had been employed there, so I had a keen interest. Journalists reported extensively on the legal battle that ensued among board members, as well as former employees.

The building had been an eyesore ever since. The roof had fallen in at one section. Most of the windows had been smashed in by kids who lobbed stones at it for fun. Ironically, the factory still had its corrugated sheeting and copper piping. Not only was it never plundered by metal thieves, but there were no reports of homeless occupants squatting in the building. In South Africa, this was almost unheard of. With an unyielding unemployment rate and soaring crime stats, vacant properties were quickly occupied by vagrants or pillaged by vandals.

Before entering the factory, Gavin stepped up to me, his nose touching mine. His eyes were fierce. The terrible monster inside of him was evaluating me carefully.

"From now on, you keep absolutely quiet."

Caution should have interjected long before this point, but it hadn't. I realized I was about to get in way over my head. After this, I would be no better than those who had wronged me, but I couldn't stop myself. I wanted justice for Brenda, my mother, Allan, and Satí, even if it came at the cost of losing my soul – or my mind. I was already a dead man anyway. In my mind, dragging drug dealers and murderers down with me seemed justified. I was no superhero. I was merely an amateur criminal hoping to eliminate professional criminals. And now, everything had already been set in motion. I had reached the point of no return. *Alea iacta est.*

We entered the building and scurried through the large floor space, sidestepping abandoned machinery and equipment, then dashed up a dirty staircase leading to an open wooden platform overlooking the shop floor. The warm and dusty atmosphere was a sharp contrast from the dank and gloomy ground floor. The wooden beams creaked as we made our way across the platform towards the office at the far end. Tiny clouds of dust spiralled in our wake, first curling around our ankles, then taking flight as we swooped through the section where administrative staff and management had once been isolated during their operating hours. It was dark and creepy, with desks and remnants of office equipment partially visible in the shadows.

Gavin's stealth capabilities were far more advanced than my own. He often glanced sideways at me when I bumped into something or stirred up dirt, a glint of annoyance in his eyes.

We were huddled inside what looked like the manager's office when Gavin finally broke his self-imposed silence.

"You stay here when they come," he whispered.

I shook my head, not sure if I was permitted to talk. He sighed and beckoned me to speak with his one hand.

"They, who?"

"The they *you* paid me to kill."

"Oh, right." I thought about it, then asked, "How sure are you they will come here?"

"You don't know much, do you? This is a dump house. A place where they store drugs."

My eyes grew wide in surprise. Detective Xhosa had mentioned how reluctant police were to take on Collins or Daniels. I realized that if the location was used for illegal activity, then everyone would know about it, and therefore avoid it, which explained why the building was still intact.

"A drug dump? How could you possibly know that?"

"Keep your voice down, will you," he shushed me, then continued, "This is one of Collins' spots. They stash their shit here. Runners distribute it to dealers from here, who in turn sell it to junkies along Voortrekker Road, from Parow, through Bellville, and into Kuils River, where they clash with Denvor's crew."

"How the hell do you know all this?" I asked.

"How do you not know it? No one can be that ignorant." He stared at me with a comical expression frozen on his face, then shook his head thoughtfully. "You live in the middle of a war zone, pal. That's what the shootouts are about. The night your brother was shot, their little turf war reached an impasse." He removed a small black pistol from one jacket pocket and a black cylindrical tube from the other. He screwed the metal tube onto the front of the pistol with a slow methodical twist of his wrist. There was a soft grating sound as he tightened the silencer. He raised the weapon and took aim across the platform, closed one eye, then the other. "Of course, you'd know all this if you bothered to take your head out your bum hole and weren't living in your perfect little suburban bubble."

"I resent that."

"Noted," he said with a wry smile. "Tell it to someone who gives a shit." He racked the slide back to chamber a round. It made a *click-clack* sound. "They are making a collection here today. Shane is present during collections because he distrusts his own crew. He only brings one or two bums along, so it should be easy enough."

"What about Denvor Daniels?" I asked.

"First Collins, then Daniels. You paid for one head. After this you pay for the second head. Agreed?"

I was about to ask how he had obtained all the specifics when Gavin held up his hand. Outside we heard cars pulling up, doors opening and closing, then voices and footsteps approaching.

"Put your game face on, Sparky," he whispered and winked at me. He handed me a grey balaclava. I consented. "Keep your mouth shut. Don't move a muscle. You only observe. You feel me?" he commanded. I nodded earnestly. "If you do anything, I'll cut you up and scatter your pieces around Zeekoevlei."

With that horrible image lodged in my mind, Gavin pulled a black balaclava over his own head. His eyes grew cold once more, as though one Gavin was stepping out, and another was stepping in. The transition was sublime. Insanity made sane. It was like watching smoke evaporate. He blew across the platform and flitted out of sight, blending into the shadows and moving along the walls like a shapeshifter. At one stage I saw shadows moving near the bottom of the staircase. I assumed he had moved along the factory floor to a predetermined spot.

CHAPTER 15

A large roller-shutter door, probably the factory's main entrance whilst in operation, grinded open as it rolled back on its track. A sharp blade of sunlight pierced the darkness and fell across the dusty floor that expanded once the door opening widened. Dust particles sparkled through the sunlight as though they were scurrying for cover. When the door stopped in its track, three men entered the building.

Shane Collins strolled in first with his unmistakable swagger. He swayed his arms and tilted his head as he moved, the same way he had after the restaurant shootout. When he whistled, it crept along the walls and echoed across the deserted shop floor. It was an eerie, menacing sound that enraged me, but it also sent shivers through me. This confusion between anger and fear kept me from doing something silly.

I later identified Collins' accomplices as Zahier Moodley and Willie Stols, his most trusted bodyguards. They walked up to a platform that had been hidden in the dark. Each man took a rope and tugged at it. A wooden section the size and shape of a single garage door was dragged across the surface of the cement floor, scraping loudly. The dark pit underneath the door slowly came into view. Zahier, the more agile of the three, clambered down a ladder which led into the pit. Before long a parcel was held out for Stols to collect, which Stols then took to the car.

"This shithole won't work for much longer," Shane said in thought. "The *bra* I'm paying off is losing the court battle. We must find another spot."

Zahier looked up at Shane from where he stood on the ladder and pulled back his sports cap. "That spot in Parow can work," he said. His voice was sharp. His words were clear and crisp. "We just have to squeeze the landlords or make it worth their while."

"Nah, that spot is too close to the crew coming up from the Southern Suburbs. Voortrekker Road is already littered with junkies and whores, so we need to think more North." Shane glanced at his watch, then looked questioningly after Sols. "Besides, we have too many bodies buried there. The coppers will dig up some of them when they start building houses."

"Ok, so what do we do?" Zahier asked as Stols trudged back into the building.

Shane kicked at something on the floor. It rolled out of sight and ricocheted off one of the machines, emitting a clanging sound that repeated itself a couple of times. I was sure I saw Gavin's boots retreating and pulling further into the darkness near the edge where the item had struck a machine.

"Let's empty it out. This place is getting too small anyway. I'm going to get a dump spot under Denvor's nose, in the heart of Kuils River. Screw him. Who wants Bellville when Kuils River is up for grabs?" He snorted and spat out a mouthful of mucus. "Come on, finish up. No double pay on Sundays."

Zahier nodded enthusiastically as Stols moved closer to

collect another parcel. Zahier tossed out another seven large parcels, climbed up the ladder and helped Stols load them into a van outside.

When Shane was alone on the shop floor, he lit a cigarette, puffed at it, and expelled a long snake of smoke that coiled out from the confinement of his lips. He circled the pit, stared into its depths, as though he was caught in a negotiation with the hole, then headed towards where I had last seen the tips of Gavin's boots. I sensed the moment of my revenge fast approaching.

I leaned closer to the edge of the platform to get a better view. My breathing became more urgent as a sense of excitement took hold of me. A film of perspiration spread across my head and a wave of nausea hit me. In fear of suffering another nervous breakdown, I considered looking away, but my head would not move. My eyes were frozen in their sockets and my eyelids could not close. Even with the balaclava, my neck was icy cold. For a split second, I wanted to call out to Shane to warn him, or to Gavin to stop him from taking the shot. It was the strangest experience. I held sway over Shane's life. That power was intoxicating.

In the shadows, I saw a glimpse of Gavin's eyes as his target approached. Knowing where to look, I made out what looked like the tip of the silencer. It was aimed at Shane's head. Gavin was poised, ready to strike. In that moment I was convinced that Gavin had military experience. I was further convinced that he would kill me after he had killed Shane.

Outside, the delivery truck's door squeaked open, then the two men began laughing. The commotion spurred Gavin to action. He drifted out of the shadows, like smoke spilling from a chimney flue. He walked up to Shane, his weapon centimetres away from the man's head. Then I heard a rattling sound behind me.

I turned towards the sound, just in time to see a dove burst into flight, leaping from the shadows as though chased from where it had been perched. Its wings cluttered loudly as it flapped its way across the empty space of the shop floor, chasing up a cloud of dust as it swooped over Gavin's head.

Shane ducked down and looked up at the dove as it twirled and arched through the intermittent beams of light. He had pulled out a gun so fast that I only noticed it after he had focused it on the bird. Gavin, in turn, had momentarily taken his eyes off Shane to examine the bird as it circled around in the closed space above them. Then he stared up at where I had been told to hide. His face hardened. Somehow, I knew he blamed me for the distraction. I hastened to the thought that my fate had been sealed; that I had inadvertently paid for my own assassination.

Gavin took a cautious step backward, but his right boot came down on the item Shane had sent spinning across the floor moments before. His foot rolled outward. He lost his balance and stumbled backward. He flipped his upper body around to stop the fall but disappeared behind the machinery where he had been hiding. As the bird swooped noisily around the building, crashing into the corrugated roof sheeting, I heard a snapping sound coming from Gavin's position, like the sound of a branch cracking, followed by a compressed puff of air. I suspected that this was the sound of Gavin's silenced weapon firing off a round, but, as I'd never heard one in use, I couldn't be sure. If it was Gavin's weapon, then it wasn't exactly Hollywood-quiet, but since it coincided with the sounds of the bird's wings and the delivery truck's doors slamming shut, it didn't rouse any suspicion from Shane. I did, however, make out a tiny yellow flash in the dark, no brighter than the glow of Shane's cigarette. But Shane was still alive. If Gavin had fired his weapon, he would have missed his target. That did not bode well for me.

Zahier and Stols returned for the remaining parcels, surprised to find Shane crouched low, gun held high.

"Boss?" asked Zahier, scanning the factory floor, his own hand sliding towards a protrusion in the small of his back.

Shane was momentarily disoriented, unsure of himself and suspicious. "I thought I heard something."

Following Shane's line of sight, Stols saw the bird diving at an obscure angle, darting through the open doorway and escaping into daylight. "It was just a bird," he said. "It's gone now."

"I know it was a bird! You think I'm blind?"

Zahier looked questioningly at Stols, who shrugged and pulled his face in mock surprise.

"There was something. Something else … Like a sound …" Shane trailed off, then slowly got to his feet. "This place gives me the creeps. Let's roll."

They left the pit open, shut the roller door and got into their cars. Gravel clanged and rattled against the metal door as they sped off. An incriminating silence roamed.

My joints were frozen stiff and my excitement from earlier had evaporated. I was exhausted by the tension of the scene I had just witnessed. My two cappuccinos from earlier that morning didn't help. I sat there in the dark for about fifteen minutes, maybe more, half-expecting Gavin to leap from the shadows and send a bullet spiralling through the tumour in my brain. Besides the sporadic cracking sounds of the roof's corrugated metal sheets shifting in the heat, there was no movement or sound.

I crept out of my hiding spot and got to my feet, smacking the dust off my pants. A part of me hoped to see Gavin standing by the pit, another part hoped never to see him again. My curiosity, on the other hand, propelled me forward, slowly, over the wooden platform, down the staircase and across the deserted factory floor. I stopped at the edge of the pit and looked down into the darkened abyss. I was overcome with vertigo when my mind revisited the various open gravesites I had seen the last couple of months.

I moved back to force myself free from the lure of the pit. In doing so, I stepped on the brass doorknob which had caused Gavin to fall. It rolled under my foot, causing me to lose my balance, then shot across the floor once more as I tipped over and collapsed to the floor. Unlike Gavin, I fell flat on my back, rousing up a cloud of dust. The air leapt from my lungs as my diaphragm flexed from the impact. I forced air into my lungs and coughed it out again. I slowly rolled over and struggled to my knees.

From the dark, two glassy eyes glared at me, judging me. At first, I couldn't move. My consternation subsided when I realized there was no life left in those mean eyes. My recent bouts with misery must have hardened my heart because I was left unfazed by the sight of a corpse spreadeagled across the machinery.

I got up and went to Gavin's body. He lay on his chest, one arm twisted around and pinned under his neck in an obscure way. I surmised that he had shot himself in the neck at an upward angle as he connected with the ground and that the bullet must have exited out his left ear. Inspecting the body to confirm my guesswork would bear no fruit. It smelled as though Gavin had defecated himself. He was clearly dead. I didn't see the sense in hanging around.

I took hold of his jacket, jerked the body free and dragged it towards the pit, leaving a dark bloody trail in the dust. It took a surprisingly long time to roll him over and into the pit. His body dropped to the bottom with a loud thud that nearly liberated the omelette breakfast from my stomach. I considered pulling the wooden platform back into place, but it wasn't a one-man job. It would just create more evidence that I had been there.

I picked up Gavin's silenced weapon and studied it. I contemplated the consequences of being caught with it in my possession. Every eventuality ended with one certainty: I was already a dead man. I was living on borrowed time and had no one to share it with.

Mid-consternation, I heard a loud rattle as the roller door shuddered back on its track. The beam of light slowly extended across the dusty floor. Zahier's long face appeared in the opening. I stood motionless beside the pit, my head covered with the grey balaclava, gun in hand.

"Gavin?" he whispered as he entered the building. "Where you at, bro?"

Zahier had hollow cheeks, a sharp nose, and deceptively comforting hazel eyes. He squinted until his keen eyes adjusted to the dark, then discerned me in the shadows. He straightened up and approached me.

"Why didn't you take the shot, man? I could've handled Stols on my own? Now we must make another plan."

I said nothing. I did not move in any way, not even my eyes.

As I watched, Zahier went down into the pit as lithely as he had before, a vapor in motion, his feet floating over the steps of the short ladder. He made a triumphant sound, then a parcel wrapped in newspaper flew out of the hole and tumbled toward me. It was the size of a five-kilogram bag of sugar.

"If I wasn't so reasonable, I'd say that cost you your cut," he called from the darkness.

Another parcel, equal in shape and size, landed near my feet. My feet shuffled back of their own accord.

A soft grating sound rose from the pit, then a slapping sound, followed by a groan. I suspect that Zahier must have tripped over Gavin's body.

"What the hell is this?" his voice called. "Gavin! There's a body down here, bro. Who'd you kill?"

I turned and ran with all my might, as silently as I could, giving heed to caution. I flew past the staff toilets, out of the rear Judas gate where Gavin and I had entered, then shot across the yard. The little Toyota didn't falter. She roared to life and spewed out bits of earth as I guided her back and out towards the gate. The car struck the pile of rotten pallets and blew it asunder. I charged through the gate, no longer concerned about my car. The lock and chain gave way easily enough, but the crunch of metal sheeting and the loud scrape of it against both doors echoed in the confines of the car. The tires screeched once they found tar. The car's backside pulled outward as I oversteered, sent sideways with centrifugal force, but I was able to regain control. I raced down the road, passing the church again on my way out. I saw no churchgoers or witnesses who could identify me or my car.

I was frantic. My mind was spinning. My vision was blurry at the edges with the same annoying white spots scattered across my periphery. My hands gripped the steering wheel so hard that I felt my nails digging into my palms. I jumbled up the gears and the Toyota flared up in disagreement. Only then did I slow down to the speed limit. It was as though the balaclava was constricting me, limiting my freedom of movement or hindering my ability to breathe. As I approached the traffic light, I pulled the balaclava from my head, but the sense of claustrophobia didn't go away. I left the Industrial area the same way I had arrived and slipped into the back roads of the Bellville suburbia. There I parked the car in a quiet side road and went home on foot, crossing a small foot bridge that led over the railway. Later that afternoon I would report the car stolen.

CHAPTER 16

"Whoa, whoa, whoa," Shane interrupted. He looked to Denvor, then to his men, then to me, his face contorted with confusion.

"What?!" he screamed after a moment's reflection. "What is this?"

He raised his gun at me, but I saw no indication that he would pull the trigger. His expression was priceless. He was being tormented by questions. He shifted his aim across the room, focusing his sights on Willie Stols and Zahier Moodley, who were glaring at each other. "You," he said to Stols, then to Zahier, "And you." He took a step towards them. "What is this?"

Stols paid no attention to Shane. "You think you can take me?" he snarled at Zahier. I had followed Stols around for months, but I had never seen his eyes blaze with fury as they did at that moment.

Denvor's chair scraped against the cemented floors when he got to his feet. Shane swung around and pointed his weapon at Denvor. "And you, too," he screamed, then to the whole room, "All of you! What is this?"

Denvor raised his hands in mock surrender to show that he

was not the threat. When Shane refocused on Zahier, Denvor glanced at Blaine Dumeko. The look that passed between them was the sum of the confusion I had sown. Dumeko shifted his bulging shoulders in confusion, though his round lips betrayed the hint of a smile.

With the effect of uncertainty in full swing, Stols and Zahier suddenly went at each other like two wild dogs. Stols wrapped his large hands around Zahier's throat and began to throttle him. He hoisted Zahier up effortlessly and pinned him to the wall, his neck in a vice grip and his eyes filled with panic. Stols was twice as strong as Zahier, but Zahier was twice as cunning. As everyone looked on, Zahier's hands fumbled about in his pockets, then the blade of his pocketknife announced its presence by its reflection in the light. Zahier made four quick jabs under Stols' left arm. With each blow, the full length of the blade poked through Stols' yellow tracksuit jacket and sunk into the flesh underneath.

A sullen silence fell over the room as Stols slowly relented his grip and collapsed to the floor next to my chair. He groaned softly and kicked at the black plastic as life slipped away from him. An obscene gurgling sound escaped Stols' throat, then his eyes glazed over, and his features tensed up. It was not the same as seeing Gavin's vacant eyes stare at me, but it was also not the first time I saw someone die up close. The first time I had stared into someone's eyes as their soul departed had been far more jarring to witness. This felt justified.

Zahier dropped to his knees, coughed and sucked in a pocket of air. Both his eyes watered as he coaxed the oxygen back into his body.

The atmosphere in the room became electric. Everyone looked at Stols' body with a type of reverence that I didn't understand. They were frozen in awe. All the men in the room had been a party to murder at some point, yet they were ensnared by wonderment now that death had finally arrived. For the briefest moment, I pitied them. Death was among them, and they were unprepared.

Shane was first to recover from the haze of uncertainty. He moved so quickly that no one could restrain him. He flew over Stols' body and helped Zahier to his feet. He put an arm around Zahier's neck, pulled him tight to his body and forced him into an embrace. Zahier grabbed hold of Shane's shirt to free himself from the hold, but Shane pressed the barrel of his gun against Zahier's chest and pulled the trigger.

The report was surprisingly quiet, but still loud enough to ripple across the faces of the men in the room. The bullet travelled through Zahier's chest cavity, blasted through the back of his sports jacket and smacked into the plaster of the wall. Zahier went limp in Shane's embrace. His fists unclenched and his long fingers trailed down Shane's sides. Shane stepped aside and let Zahier's body drop over that of Stols.

"Are you mental?!" Denvor screamed at him. "This is my house."

Shane scrutinized Denvor from the distant realms of his insanity, his body trembling in delight. I noticed how he was tapping the barrel of the gun against his pants and wondered how close he was to shooting Denvor at that moment. Their little 'war' had been mostly for show, and with the threat of opposition pushing into their territory, there had been hopes of reconciliation. However, after both Harry's and Zahier's betrayal, Shane seemed to be backed into a corner. His inner beast was stirring.

"Oh, shut up, will you? I didn't choose this location."

"Police can trace gunshots," Denvor continued.

"That is a good reason not to shit where you eat, Denvor. You never learn, *bra*." He pointed at the heap of bodies. "You do this in a secluded area."

"The coppers have me under eye and you know it. They are crawling all over my hangouts. Yours as well."

"You worry too much, *bra*. The shot spotters detect unmuzzled gunshots. This was no louder than the renovations you're doing here on your little spank pad."

"It's still a risk," Denvor said, regaining his composure.

"Risk?" He stepped over the expanding pool of blood. "And where would we be without risk? We built an empire on risk."

"There is no more *we*, Shane. I run an enterprise, not a circus. That's *your* game."

Shane stepped closer to Denvor, the barrel tapping against his leg. "False confidence like that can get your knees capped."

"Careful. Your workforce is down by three," Denvor cautioned. "You're outnumbered here. You try that again and I'll put you in a grave where my dog takes his morning dump."

"Don't goad me, *bra*. I can get another fifty guys here in ten minutes."

"Yeah? So why don't you call them?" Shane wavered for a second too long, so Denvor continued, "You know me well enough to know I don't make empty threats. We called a truce today. This was to find out who is making the move on both our businesses. Not just mine. Don't make me regret it."

Shane stopped tapping the gun against his leg, recalculating the way forward. The beast retreated and the playful smile returned to his face.

"Truce. Indeed. Then let's get back to it." He came around to face me. He pressed the gun to my scalp, more to annoy Denvor than to scare me. It was the very spot where Dr. Immelman had pressed his finger to indicate the location of the tumour. "What's your story, hey? Who are you really, Mr. Gray?" he asked.

The barrel was warm against my skin, but not as warm as I had imagined it would be.

"I told you before, my name is just Gray, not Mr. Gray."

"I'll call you whatever I want. You understand me." He leaned over until his eyes floated opposite mine. "I don't know what game you are playing, but I have a secret for you. You're never going to make it out of this room alive, *bra*." He came even closer, until his lips almost touched my right ear, then whispered, "You are already a ghost. You just don't know it yet." He came around again to see if his words had found purchase. It hadn't.

"You are not listening. You took me from my home against my will, remember? You abducted me."

Shane relented and moved back to his table, saying, "only because my contacts pinned you as one of the *okes* from Rondebosch. They said you were bribing dealers in Parow. But that's not true, is it? The Parow crew was working with the coppers. Informants. We know that. And we took special care of them, too." When I didn't answer, Shane offered Denvor a pleading look. "The *bra* is a nobody, man. He knows nothing. He's trouble."

"You're not thinking straight, Shane. There's something else going on here. He knows too much about our dealings to be a nobody. I want to know who he is working for."

Shane scoffed at Denvor, then asked, "What type of name is Gray, anyway?"

I thought about that for a moment. My eyes must have revealed that I was rummaging through a basket of tired memories because both men were staring at me.

"Gray is a unit used to measure energies associated with radiation, like gamma or nuclear particles," I said. "One Gray is the absorption of one joule of energy per kilogram of matter."

Shane looked as though his lollipop had fallen in the sand. He turned to Denvor. "Does that answer your question? You see what I mean? He knows nothing."

Denvor stood motionless in front of the windows. Having watched him for months, I knew this was the quiet before the storm. This was when he was at his most dangerous. I sensed that Shane knew it, too, which is why he pulled back to his corner where he could review his dealings with Stols and Zahier over the last couple of months.

"You lost us, gamma boy," Shane muttered.

"It's what they pumped through my body every week. It's the invisible rays that pulverized my body while doctors quibbled over how to buy me more time."

I experienced an unusual wave of relief. Before that moment, I had never spoken about my illness or the treatment thereof. I had no one to share my pain and suffering with. I had faced the ordeal of cancer alone.

"Time?" Denvor asked. "Time for what?"

I didn't answer. We looked at each other for a long time.

"Time to arrange this encounter?" he persisted.

Again, I didn't answer. I could see the mechanisms working behind Denvor's eyes. He was deciding whether to let me finish, or whether to put me down.

"Alright, Gray," he said finally. "Get on with it."

The room was silent, listening intently to what the soon-to-be corpse sitting in the chair had left to say.

CHAPTER 17

"As mentioned previously, your cancer is inoperable because it's present in both the left and right cerebral hemispheres as metastatic brain tumours. I wouldn't classify it as interlobular, but that's a more technical view." Andre Immelman spoke in a calm, neutral tone. "It's even spread to the spinal cord with secondary tumour colonies already established around the brainstem. I'm afraid there's no quick fix when glioblastoma is this advanced. I'm so sorry to lay it out so bluntly, but I've found this to be the best approach. Sensitivity and the NURSE mnemonic can only guide me so far as a physician, but the reality is that you are facing death head-on and there is very little that I can do to help you through this journey. There are specialized treatment options to control tumour growth that could prolong your life, but not by much."

In the silence that followed, I stared out the windows. The trunk of a tall palm tree was swaying from side to side as the wind tugged at its branches. It resembled a metronome, consistent and resolute in the way it defied nature's relentless push and pull.

Immelman's office was a place of comfort. The iced coffee-coloured paint on the walls added a calming quality to the room. There were two floor planters topped with white pebbles, one containing a small Delicious Monster and the other a bright green bamboo palm. I sat on the brown couch where other patients had sat before me – and will sit long after I had passed away.

"What type of treatment?"

"There aren't many options," he said.

He sat opposite me, but it felt as though he was sitting next to me, holding my hand. He had a notepad open on his lap. One hand was curled over his chin as though he was deep in thought. I found reassurance in his presence. Somehow this was helping me to digest my imminent death.

"The golden standard is to do chemo and radiation therapy as a concurrent treatment, with the aim to stop further growth. Doing both at the same time will be very invasive to your system, but it has some benefits when facing an advanced or aggressive cancer." He handed me a leaflet about curcumin IV drip therapy. "We can look at a variety of intravenous drips that have been quite effective in slowing down tumour growth. Studies show that turmeric can decrease the malignant characteristics of GBM. There are also some cannabinoid treatments that are still in trial phases, but the results of CBD look very promising. These are only suggestions. Ideally, you must choose a treatment you are comfortable with."

"How bad will this get?"

"That all depends," Andre said. He shifted, grimaced and put the notepad aside. "Have you had any spells?"

"Spells?"

"Do you find yourself doing or saying things that you normally wouldn't?"

I pictured my reflection in Brenda's cracked mirror; my body covered in dark earth. "I'm not sure if this is what you mean, but my memory is not as crisp as before. Sometimes it takes me a while to disentangle a specific memory."

"Yes, some encounter forgetfulness, others experience bouts of hysteria. It can go either way when the brain is involved. These spells could become more frequent and often more intense, taking patients to a previously unexplored space where they are risk averse. This can make them awkward, erratic, and even dangerous. I've seen it bring out the absolute worst in someone. In rare cases, it can lead to dramatic neurobehavioral symptoms, like personality disorders, dissociation and hallucinations. So, if you start hearing or seeing things that aren't there, you're in trouble."

Somewhere in the hidden depths of my soul, something sinister fluttered. While this hinted at a lingering menace unbeknown to me, my only concern at that moment was the memory of Brenda. If it was my fate to wither away and to race into a grave, then I would grudgingly oblige, but I aspired to do so without spoiling the memories of my late wife.

"Is there a way to curb these spells?"

"Constant sedation might aid, but it really comes down to the individual. Everyone reacts differently. Normally I'd suggest surrounding yourself with close family or friends. In your case, I'd advise getting a personal assistant or nurse to help you attain your daily goals. It's also not a bad idea to scale down your lifestyle. You know, make your life less complicated, more manageable."

He sat with me for two hours. We discussed all the procedures and possible outcomes. They sounded grim, though it offered me perspective. Emotions came and went at will, ranging from depression to stoicism. At one point I burst into tears, the next I laughed.

While Andre was incredibly easy to talk with, I refrained from sharing details about the onset of my woes. I did not name the wrongdoers who had complicated my life, nor did I lay bare my plans for revenge. That was a private marsh I had waded into by accident and there was no hope of extricating myself from it. I only had to remain alive long enough to exact my vengeance.

We both agreed that chemoradiotherapy was the most aggressive option available and that the desired result was to win a couple of months. The treatment was scheduled to start the following day. I was not looking forward to it.

When I returned home, I contacted Bob Sampson with the terrible, wonderful news of my diagnosis. I submitted the doctor's findings and informed him that my life insurance policy had a sizable lump sum Dreaded Disease benefit, which would pay out if I was diagnosed with a critical illness, like brain cancer. The Income Protector benefit added to the policy enabled me to claim a salaried income for as long as the disease inhibited my ability to work. My fortune kept growing as my sorrows doubled. My cart's wheels sunk deeper into the mire and my yoke became unbearable.

Bob was unable to tell me anything about Bertie September. He had logged calls to find out who had assigned an investigator to my file. We both suspected that the investigation could be the result of new legislation tabled by the South African Revenue Service, which meant that Bertie was probably contracted by the government to hunt for estate duty tax evaders. He confirmed that half of the initial investments had paid out and that he would invest the full amount into a high-risk cryptocurrency asset investment, which was the most volatile investment he could think of. I gave him my approval. I didn't care about the money. I would never get to spend it. I could burn through the R50 million by buying cars and property, but what good would that do me? I was moderation personified. I have never lived beyond my means, so why would I embrace extravagance now? I risked little and kept to myself. The money was more aggravating than the execrable tumour expanding across the grey matter of my brain. I didn't want a single cent of it. I wanted my life back. I wanted Brenda back.

I played with the idea of letting Detective Xhosa know that his referral had met a gruesome end but decided against it. Instead, I continued my surveillance efforts alone. The one thing that my encounter with Gavin had taught me was that I knew nothing about those who had caused my sorrow. Xhosa had mentioned locations favoured by Collins and Daniels. Since my diary was empty, I began staking out those addresses. I had no desire to explore the myth of inner peace or to discover the true meaning of life while being held captive in the throes of death. Between chemoradiotherapy appointments, I could devote whatever time and energy remained to understanding the operations of the two men who ruled the drug industry in the northern suburbs of Cape Town.

With money no longer a concern, I bought a blue Honda hatchback to conduct my surveillance work. I had reported the Toyota stolen, and, sure enough, the police recovered it a week later. An insurance assessor explained that someone must have taken the car for a joyride through town because the hood of the car and the undercarriage suffered extensive damage. The car was not technically a write-off, so the insurance company paid to have it repaired. Once repaired, the car served as a trade-in for the Honda. It felt liberating to do something as mundane as buying a car, a task that would have previously taken me ages to finalize. Life had been unconventional of late.

After I visited the doctor, I went to a coffee shop that overlooked an intersection where Kuils River and Brackenfell merged. I was advised to reduce my food intake in preparation for the treatment, so I ordered a light lunch. I sat outside so I could keep my sunglasses on without arousing suspicion. I kept to myself, browsed through newspapers, studied the chemoradiotherapy leaflets and flicked through my social media feeds, while my eyes inspected the building on the opposite side of the road.

I sat in the exact spot where Detective Xhosa's daughter had been shot. Through old newspaper articles, I was able to deduce what had happened. Detective Xhosa had rented out the coffee shop for the evening to do a pre-wedding supper. After Lindiwe Xhosa arrived, a car with tinted windows raced by. Gunfire erupted. The target had been the building on the other side of the road. The returning gunfire aimed at the moving car riddled the front display of a refrigeration company next to the coffee shop. One stray bullet ricocheted off a metal signboard and struck Lindiwe in the throat. After numerous operations, she died while in a coma two months later.

Lindiwe's picture in the local newspaper was of her at the university where she had been studying. In the picture, she had an infectious smile, the type of smile that poured out of someone's eyes and made others smile. I couldn't help thinking that the world was worse off for having lost one of those beautiful faces and intoxicating smiles. I reasoned, as I sipped my coffee, that if we kept erasing those smiles, there would soon be little left to live for. The innocents, the ones who succumbed to the burden of crime, were the bearers of joy, compassion and purity. They were supposed to be our fruits. They were in decline. They were the endangered few, the easy prey.

It was a fruitless day. I felt like an amateur sleuth. I had no clue how to find the people responsible for my loss. I had little to go on. The Kuils River building, as well as the abandoned Bellville factory, were the only places I could investigate with the hope of getting leads. However, there lingered a reluctance inside of me. Deep down, I first wanted to face my cancer treatment. There was little sense in delaying the inevitable. I wanted to buy time. Without time, my reconnaissance was pointless. I resolved to return the day after my first round of treatment, not knowing what awaited me.

CHAPTER 18

The preparation guide described chemotherapy as an invasive drug treatment that hindered a cancer cell's ability to divide, reproduce and grow in a body. Radiation therapy, on the other hand, seemed exciting on the page. A radiation therapist would aim an external beam at my head and zap the tumour inside my brain with no more than 60 Gray (Gy), which is the maximum amount of radiation used in the treatment of advanced brain cancer. The process sounded uncomplicated, almost self-explanatory. Chemo would stop cancer's rate of growth and radiation would break it up. Andre Immelman cautioned me not to be hopeful about remission after the procedure. He said it would take a small miracle for a tumour that advanced to break up to a degree as to make it operable—and miracles were in short supply.

The nurses shuffled about in the private clinic's waiting room with despair-fuelled lethargy. Their smiles were sincere, but their faces looked tired. Their eyes hid the grim reality of their occupation. They were angels bidden to a task that few had the nerve to execute.

Not even the décor or the soft classical music tickling my eardrums could extinguish the overwhelming presence of death that awaited patients at the cancer treatment facility. Within those walls, death took on a completely different guise, one that took me by surprise. Contrary to that of a black-clad grim reaper with a shiny bladed scythe in hand, I encountered a Death that was clinically clean, ghostly white and as sanitary as sin. He welcomed me in the foyer and showed me around with an eerie grin on his hollow features. He stared down at me from the ceiling when the nurse administered my intravenous drip, which fed the chemotherapy drugs into my veins. He gawked at me over the shoulder of the young radiation therapist who fired off laser beams at the beast growing inside my head. Then he bid me farewell as the clinic door slid shut behind me. And there he remained, counting off the days to my next visit.

I sat in the Honda with my arms extended, hands clasping the steering wheel, and my thoughts running wild. Something felt different in my body, but I couldn't put a finger on it. I was jittery, though I attributed that to white coat syndrome. While I thought I was being paranoid, my body kept tensing up. It felt as though my body was rebelling against the early onset of flu. The experience was so profound that I put my surveillance efforts on hold for the day and returned home. To appease the sudden lunchtime hunger pangs, I bought a hamburger midway. I devoured it on the couch and fell into a deep sleep while the TV, my only companion, prattled on in the background.

As deep as it was, my sleep was plagued by terrible dreams and visions that I am unable to recall. There must have been some harrowing stuff swirling around my imagination, because when I woke up the couch was soaked through with sweat. I shivered all over, but my body was hot and sticky. I had no recollection of time, but it was dark outside. I had a quick shower. It didn't help.

I crept into bed and tried to go to sleep, but my body had other plans. Then my stomach began to lurch furiously. It pushed up into my chest, which made me heave. I rolled out of bed and headed to the bathroom but was overcome by an intense dizzy spell. My hands searched wildly for support, something solid to hold on to, but found nothing. I stumbled sideways, lost control of my body in the process, and spewed out chunks of meat and hamburger bun across the floor.

The rest of the night or early morning hours was a furious battle between me and whoever, or whatever, had taken control of my body. It not only had full control over my bodily functions, but it randomly selected which functions to hijack and when to do so. An alien being had taken occupancy while I had been absent. It had unfolded in my body, tentacles curling down the length of each limb and up my spine. It could press my nerves, pinch my tendons and instruct my brain to empty my bladder or my bowels at the most inappropriate times. At around 11 AM the next morning, after undergoing hours of torture, I was spat out by this occupying force. I was an empty shell called Gray.

I quickly realized that I needed some items to accommodate this part of the treatment process that no one had cautioned me about. Cleaning up and getting dressed took ages, as did getting to the store in one piece. I was so exhausted from retching that I was unable to hold onto the steering wheel. About two blocks from the store, I slew into a parking bay demarcated exclusively for buses. The rap of a traffic officer's knuckles against my window drew me from my confused slumber. His skin had the smooth texture of darkened caramel and he smelled incredibly clean, like the pre-treatment scrub they used at the clinic. His teeth were perfectly aligned and brilliantly white.

I have no idea what I told him. I only remember his sympathetic grimace and how his hardened eyes softened. He asked if I needed medical assistance. I declined. Then he leaned into my window, put the Honda's hazards on and told me to close the window and lock the doors until I felt better. As the window rolled shut, I saw the man wave a bus on to a different parking space where occupants debussed, and other passengers embussed.

I eventually made it to the shops. At the chemist I found a round-faced assistant who had once been a locum nurse in a cancer ward. She accompanied me through the aisles, pointing out things that would be of use. The need for incontinence wear was a bitter obstacle for me to make peace with. She advised me to create a little chemo bag, which I systematically filled with things as the consequences of the treatment became known to me over the coming days. I later added emesis bags for when I had to throw up, sanitary wipes, adult nappies, lip balm, medication for nausea and pain, bottled water, and a facecloth. She suggested I keep a change of clothing and other contingencies in the car, which I made a mental note of. She had a pleasant way about her, a reassuring calmness that resonated from within. When I became faint, she offered me her arm and took my hand in hers, stroking it slowly. She led me along the bollard, through the till point and escorted me out to my car, where we parted ways. She had shown me how to order items and pay online, which would make things easier for both of us.

I battled through the next two days as I tried to adjust to the unpleasantness of chemoradiation. It became a form of acceptance, which was the grey area where resistance and submission converged. Three days after being subjected to my first cancer treatment, a modicum of clarity reached through the haze.

I recalled the wrongs I was compelled to right while I was still alive. An entirely different revenge reclaimed its hold on me and waged war with the lingering effects of my treatment. I no longer had a burning desire to repay death for death. Something had changed, though I couldn't put my finger on it. I began doubting my approach to the exercise of revenge. Though I must admit that this feeling of uncertainty came and went. I decided to give myself an ultimatum. I'd try one more time to locate either Denvor Daniels or Shane Collins. If my efforts held no fruit, I was not meant to pursue my transgressors.

Once more, I took up my position at the coffee shop in Kuils River. It was a Friday afternoon. The traffic trickled along the main road and people milled about. Toxic fumes from a nearby factory arrested the smell of my coffee and drove me to nausea. Pedestrians and fellow patrons appeared to harbour a longing for the weekend. I was simply trying to forget the last couple of days.

I ate and drank according to what my body cautioned me would be least likely to be expelled. A pie with chips, rooibos tea and loads of water was all I could stomach. The hours drifted by as the sun was slung across the sky. Later that afternoon, after another dizzy spell came and went, I began to make peace with the fact that revenge was probably not on the cards.

I was about to call it a day when two luxury sedans crept into my periphery. I saw a man alight to the curb near the entrance of the building. It was Denvor Daniels. He looked the same way I remembered him from the night Allan had been shot. He moved smoothly, almost elegantly, as though he was a celebrity hiding from paparazzi. There were three men and a scantily clad woman with him.

I hurriedly made notes in a hardcover notebook. I took down car license numbers, made descriptions of everyone and what role I imagined each person had in the life of Denvor Daniels. One of the men was none other than Blaine Dumeko. At the time I called him Daniels' Man #2. The woman I later called Daniels' Woman #2.

CHAPTER 19

"Woman number 2?" Shane winked at Denvor and said, "Nice."

"Piss off," Denvor fired back.

For the first time since I'd been placed in that chair, I noticed true resentment in Denvor's eyes. I suspect his disfavour was attributed to the fact that he had no idea how far my surveillance had taken me. I did sense a mild curiosity in him, a flutter of intrigue.

"Is that where you stash your weekend special, *bra*? On the edge of town? No wonder you don't want to share Kuils River with anyone else."

"Mind your own business, Shane, and I'll mind mine."

"Nah, *bra*, this just got interesting. We all have a *motjie* on the side, don't we?" He laughed as he raised his voice, using the derogatory term for a mistress like a blunt knife. "Mrs. Daniels number 2. I like that." Shane turned to me. "What more do you have? Tell me there is a woman number 3?"

"Shut up!" Denvor screamed. "My wife's upstairs."

As the words took shape, his face tightened with regret and his lips pulled into a thin line that cut his words short.

"Oh-oh, *motjie* number one doesn't know about *motjie* number two, does she?" Shane asked in mock surprise. He burst into laughter, genuine hilarity that chilled the marrow in my bones.

There were only two of the five men left who had accompanied Shane into the room that morning. The absence of Spicks, Stols and Moodley didn't derail Shane's alarming confidence one bit. I had come to appreciate the fact that Shane had only one fear: prison. The direst confrontations held little sway over his decision-making. The five men with Denvor, on the other hand, were not as loyal as he imagined. Following the death of Shane's brother, Macky, both operations had hit a frail patch.

I cast a quick look over the men in the room and felt a tinge of remorse for those who had died and those about to die. While relaying my cancer ordeal, the bodies of Zahier Moodley and Willie Stols had been removed from the room. The men tasked with removing the bodies were all reluctant to leave the room in fear that they would miss anything that could be relevant to them, perhaps afraid that a similar fate awaited them once they returned to the room. They had rolled both bodies in plastic and pulled them down the corridor into a backroom, where I have no doubt Harry Spicks' body still waited to be transported via car boot to an unmarked grave.

I thought briefly about Astrid Spickerman, Harry's aunt living in Grahamstown, who had no idea what her nephew had been involved in. I thought about Carmen Moodley, who had cut herself off from her only son because of his drug dealing activities. I thought about Willie Stols' brother, Damian, a postal worker and family man in the Northern Cape. I thought long and hard about all of them because it felt as though a part of me knew them or could at least relate to them in some way. The team of private investigators I had used to source all this information had all worked independently, one having no idea what the other had been researching. I had made it my ambition not only to research the people in this room, but also the innocents in their lives, the ones who were undeserving of the consequences of their illicit actions.

Brian White, Vuyo Jola, Errol Davids, Malique and Blaine Dumeko all stared at Denvor with uncertain expressions plastered on their faces. They had the upper hand in numbers, yet I could question their alliance. Shane's self-assurance, on the other hand, was so intoxicating that Manny "Plankies" Bredenkamp and Dillon Moyana stood proudly on either side of the door that led to the corridor. Both feet planted, hands overlapping their crotches; Plankies and Moyana looked ready to kill without hesitation.

It was Dumeko who broke the silence when I shifted in my chair. I might have cleared my throat to spur them on.

"Boss, we must stop this now. This guy …" He trailed off, mumbled something in Xhosa, then stared at me and shook his head. "There's something off about him. This whole thing … It doesn't feel right."

Denvor didn't reply. He gave Dumeko an unconvinced look. Then his demeanour changed. It said that he was the boss, the one calling the shots, and he was not subject to the people working for him.

"So now that your boss gets a jab, you want to put an end to it," Shane said. "Be brave, Dumi. Let's push on and hear what this *bra* has to say. Come on you." Shane kicked the side of my chair, then kicked my one leg. "Tell us more. Give us some more dirt."

CHAPTER 20

That day at the coffee shop signalled the start of an extensive surveillance assignment that lasted more than three months.

I applied the same scrutiny to the illicit operations and personal lives of Shane Collins and Denvor Daniels, including the men closest to them. I rotated from one to the other, only taking off when I went for my treatments. I was consistent and methodical in my record keeping. Zahier Moodley became a ten-page folder detailing who exactly he was and how he fit into the bigger picture within Collins's organization.

I met with Detective Xhosa in secret to know more about the feud between the two. I found that the R300, known as the Kuils River Freeway, was the dividing barrier between Collins's and Daniels's drug operations. Collins operated chiefly in Bellville, Durbanville and Parow. He encountered resistance from big operators when he pushed further south into Goodwood. Daniels owned Kraaifontein, Brackenfell and Kuils River. He also met resistance when he pushed further down into Delft or Blue Downs. Because the lines blurred in Kraaifontein and Durbanville, primarily around Langeberg and Goedemoed, skirmishes between dealers and users became commonplace, resulting in stabbings or shootings. If a dealer wandered into opposition territory, they were executed gangland-style the following day. The police were understaffed and faced logistical and regional obstacles, so they were unable to curb the increase in bodies being dumped on the outskirts of Blue Downs and Belhar. When the local police finally escalated the matter, it had got out of control. Collins and Daniels were taking serious retaliatory shots at each other across the R300. Assassination attempts and drive-by shootings occurred often. Early on, Xhosa confided in me that he had been trying to get an informant to infiltrate one of the gangs, but he never got that far. His informants were either too scared to snitch, or they were always kept at a safe operational distance.

The more notes I made, the more I realized that both operations only had a few key players. Daniels had five trusted generals who did his bidding and waged war with opposition. The others were all hapless foot soldiers who followed orders. Collins' operation also relied on five men, of whom only two now remained. I suspect Collins stuck to this operational or hierarchical structure because he copied it from Daniels and didn't have the insight to design his own, hence the reason why there were twelve men to focus my attention on.

I took pictures of everyone and followed them to their homes. I followed their wives to school and took down descriptions of their children, their parents, their aunts and uncles, and so on. I immersed myself in their lives until I knew as much as I could without making myself known to them. I lost a lot of days to my cancer treatments. Every time I went for chemoradiation, I would lose the following two days. As mentioned, I had to employ private investigators to further my efforts. Whatever the entire exercise cost me in the end, I doubled through interest earnings in a single month.

By this time, I had lost most of my hair. I began shedding a week or two after the first treatment, little tufts on the pillows or clogging around the shower drain. My gums bled when I brushed my teeth, and my sleeping patterns varied between catatonic and chaotic. My intestines were a mess after each procedure. I had little to no bladder control and suffered severe stomach cramps. My kidneys were put to task by the loads of prescribed medication. My eyes became viscous discs set in gaunt sockets and my cheeks hollowed out. My skin became so thin I could see the network of veins running beneath it.

I remember coming home from one treatment session to find Bertie September in my garden. He gave me that forced smile that looked more like a Dobermann baring its teeth. I was particularly vulnerable that day and had no energy left. My body was a bag of dried bones. Even my mind was exhausted. I couldn't deal with this guy. There was no space for him in my life. So, I invited him into my house.

A broad blade of dull daylight fell into the living room. Whether due to the time of day, the approaching rains, or because of my treatments, the sun had been robbed of its yellow intensity from the week before. It brought little to no warmth to the house and cast wayward shadows in places that Sheba and Moscow used to occupy.

"Since no one believes my theories, I've taken it upon myself to follow you around a bit," he said as he repositioned himself on the couch. He did this about five times until he was perfectly cantered on the couch, both hands crossed over his crotch.

"Oh, did you now?" I asked.

"Indeed. I know what you've been up to."

His voice was so annoying that it grated my innards. Every word drove a shard of glass into my reasoning. It was even more annoying than listening to a recording of my own voice.

"I'm going to need a tea for this," I said with an unambitious sigh. I went into the kitchen, moving slowly because of the pain in my stomach and my head. "You game?"

"Of course," Bertie replied in a neutral tone, his eyes inspecting every crevice.

My mind crawled from its stagnation and considered the scenario I found myself in. I had no idea to what extent he had investigated me. Had he really been following me around? Strange that while I was investigating the true culprits, this guy was investigating me. The irony did not escape me. I wondered if I had made mistakes that I hadn't been aware of. If someone like Bertie could discover what I was up to, then so could Collins or Daniels.

I gave Bertie a sideways glance from where I stood waiting for the kettle to boil. He was cleaning out one ear with his pinkie finger, then smelled the wax on his fingertip. He frowned, pulled up his nose, and made a gagging sound. He removed a checkered handkerchief from his cream-colored jacket and methodically polished his pinkie finger until he was satisfied.

"What else do you know?" I called from the kitchen.

"I know about your chemotherapy treatment," he said without looking up.

"Chemoradiotherapy," I corrected him. "And you'd know about that if you followed the dreaded disease claims process on my insurance profile. I suspect that information will be in the public domain, so to speak."

"True. I also know about your visit to the glass factory in Bellville," he said matter-of-factly.

He had my attention. I tried to be as casual as possible, setting out cups and pouring water into them. My hands were trembling. My heart rate was spiking. A brief dizzy spell came over me but subsided when I looked across the room at Bertie.

He sat there on my couch, by himself, inside my house, and he was annoying me. My death was imminent, so I had nothing left to lose. If something were to happen to Bertie while in my house, it would not alter my immediate future in the least. I could always claim that I was legally insane when I killed him. Cruel and terrible things began to revolve in the deserted plains of my mind. Bertie didn't strike me as an innocent party to this anymore. He was no longer there as an insurance investigator. He had nefarious intent, which stirred my annoyance.

"I'm confused." I put a cup of tea and a box of cookies down on the small table in front of him. "If you've been watching me, then you know I'm not engaged in insurance fraud."

"Indeed." He dipped his finger in the tea as before and pulled up his nose. "I think we both know this is no longer about insurance."

"Then what's this about? What are you doing here?" I walked back to the kitchen to get my own cup of tea.

"Given the current state of things, I see an opportunity. I'd be foolish not to explore or take advantage of the situation."

I was engaging in chit-chat with Bertie one moment and holding Gavin's silenced weapon the next. When I looked down and noticed the black metal of the gun extending from my hand, I was surprised. At some point, I had slipped into my bedroom and removed the weapon from my cupboard without even being aware of it.

"Oh, you have been a busy boy," Bertie said as I returned to the living room, teacup in one hand, gun in the other.

I put down the cup next to his cup, then sat down on the couch opposite him with the weapon aimed at his chest. He seemed unfazed.

"What are you hoping to achieve by investigating Mr. Collins or Mr. Daniels?" he asked.

"I have no idea," I answered. "At first, I wanted to know why. Why they did what they did. I wanted to see if they had the capacity for regret. But they don't. It's just business for them. My wife and my brother were simply in the way."

Bertie's eyes became distant as though he was attempting to understand my reasoning, then shook his head.

Outside I heard birds squabbling over something at the end of the property. I had neglected my garden for the last couple of months. The flower beds were riddled with weeds and the overgrown grass had turned yellow due to lack of irrigation. The house was too big for me to maintain. I was also too weak to maintain it. The previous week I had handed my notice to the landlord. He had agreed to let me move on without any costs. This house was also too familiar to me. Memories of Brenda haunted me. The anniversary of Brenda's death was fast approaching, which added an emotional weight to every memory. I couldn't cope with it anymore. Whatever endurance I had after her death had been stripped clear during my therapy sessions. I had to move on. Besides, I wanted to move closer to the treatment centre in the southern suburbs.

"That seems silly," Bertie said after a while. "Is there not another way to attain clarity or even peace?"

I lifted the weapon higher up until I could see his round face at the receiving end of the silencer tube. I pictured the bullet flying out into the space between us, crossing the divide, smacking into his skull and splattering the couch red and grey with brain matter, but I couldn't pull the trigger. My finger was there, poised over the sharp crook of the lever, but I could not bring the mechanisms of it to the point of firing off a round. The more I laboured at the idea of shooting, the more a layer of perspiration came over me. I had been convinced that I harboured murder in my heart, yet I couldn't execute it. Deep down I realized that if I pulled the trigger, the bullet would cause more damage to the couch than to Bertie. I really liked that couch.

"You wish to kill me? I had you all wrong in the beginning. I know now you don't have it in you to kill someone."

I relented and rested the weapon on the couch beside me. "You don't know me at all. You have no idea what I'm capable of."

"I know you better than you think. You haven't taken someone's life." He leaned back into the couch. "Not yet anyway."

"Listen, man, what do you want from me? Why are you following me? And why are you here?"

Bertie snapped into a different persona, as if he had stumbled onto a distant memory.

"Oh, of course. I almost forgot," he said and began rummaging through his leather satchel. "I want a million Rands transferred to this account." He slid a piece of paper across the coffee table and offered me an apologetic smile. "One million for my silence. I know money is not a problem for you, so there you go."

"Money?" I asked. "This is all about money?"

"Isn't it always?" he said, closing his satchel and rising to his feet. "Nice doing business with you." He turned and headed for the door, his pant legs chafing loudly against one another. The sound of the door banging shut reverberated through the house like a gunshot through an empty building.

A part of me wanted to kill Bertie. I felt and pictured things that would have been beyond me earlier that year. More than anything, I didn't want Bertie to hinder my investigation. I had little time left. Even with treatments, I only had months or even weeks remaining, which could change any second. After every scan, the red X on my calendar was pushed ahead by a couple of weeks. The rest of the week I replayed Bertie's visit and contemplated what to do. In my state of physical fragility and mental instability, I had no capacity to deal with additional stresses. I decided to pay Bertie for his silence and to continue with my plans. To shift around that sum of money without drawing suspicion meant going to see my adviser again.

Bob was a bit overwhelmed when he saw me. I probably looked like death incarnate: bald head and hollowed-out cheeks. He became overly sensitive. He got his secretary to serve us water and coffee. He asked if I was comfortable, whether the light was too bright. I dismissed his efforts and said I looked worse than I felt, which was a lie. I was constantly battling nausea and incontinence. I wanted to conclude money matters and leave the office.

Bob told me that the crypto-asset investments had trebled in the last five months because of digital currency developments in

South America, China, and the United States of America. This good news was terrible. My financial gains were marred by my emotional losses, but the gains kept on coming. My total investment portfolio was estimated at R157 million. At the mention of the amount my stomach muscles contracted, putting my adult nappies to task. Bob noticed the smell but composed himself admirably. He advised me to take it all out while the market soared, settle the tax payable to the South African Revenue Services and to reinvest elsewhere. I told him to do as he thought best.

I asked Bob about the insurance investigator, but he said there was no agent assigned to my files through conventional insurance platforms. He was adamant that I had nothing to worry about, because all the claims had paid out unattested within a year of the first claim. He informed me that my unique scenario had been included as a case study for new agents. He said that beyond the police reports of my family, there was nothing left to investigate – unless I was planning something illegal. I told him I needed money to acquire accommodation closer to the treatment facilities. I loosened a couple of million Rands, left my financial adviser's office and drove straight home. The nappy had been insufficient. Some faecal matter had made its way through. There was a chemical smell in my stool that repelled me. It was an uncomfortable, squishy drive home. The pants, my favourite pair of jeans Brenda had bought me, had to be thrown away.

I cleaned myself and went to bed, though it was still afternoon. I browsed for ground-level apartments close to the treatment centre. I contacted local real estate agents, found something I liked and arranged for payment to be made over the coming days.

I finally took Bertie's note out and studied it. I created the beneficiary as per the instructions on the paper and made the payment. I had to increase my daily limit telephonically to process a one million Rand payment, but I yielded to his demands. I paid Bertie for his silence, still not knowing exactly who he was or what the money would be used for.

CHAPTER 21

I realized that my research expedition was hitting a wall at every turn. Before his untimely demise, Gavin had spoken about drug dumps across town where both gangs stored their product. I was beginning to question my ability as an amateur sleuth. With Bertie off my back, I decided to follow the key players with more diligence to find the location of these dump sites.

This meant exposing myself more than before. I was no longer considering all the risks involved. At times I had an insane clarity, but then there were foggy moments where nothing I did made any sense. I was also in two minds about whether to take Gavin's gun along on my excursions. The incident at the abandoned glass factory in Stikland offered little confidence in my abilities as a gunman. I remember standing in front of the mirror one sunny afternoon, looking down at the gun in my hand, my white fingers wrapped around the cold metal butt and thinking, *What's the worst that can happen?* I opted to conclude my investigative work without the weapon, just an unarmed civilian snooping around.

One night I followed Blaine Dumeko and Errol Davids to a

pub on the outskirts of Kraaifontein. With my hoodie up and my jeans low, I fit right in. They were huddled around a table in the back. I sat near the edge of the bar sucking at a beer bottle. For about an hour I played chess on my phone, acting the part of a local barfly. I avoided eye contact with the barman and the bouncer, who was an obscenely large man with the brim of a flat cap pulled low over his brows.

I was about to call it a night when Dumeko and Davids left with a jittery nobody named Lloyd in tow. Over the last couple of weeks, Lloyd had become a familiar face in Denvor's crew. He was the new guy in the fold, the devoted soldier climbing the ranks, earning his seat at the big-boy table. Lloyd looked like an addict at first glance, when in fact, it was just an ever-present nervous twitch. That night, though, his face looked a bit more sunken than usual, and his eyes suggested that he was under duress. Dumeko had one muscular arm slung over Lloyd's scrawny shoulders, pulling him close as he guided him through the front gate and into the night.

As the gate closed behind them, I heard Dumeko's deep voice carry over the music. I only caught half a sentence, but it was enough to spur me on. "…and get to the dump before it's too late."

I waited until they were gone, dug out a couple of notes and slid it across the sticky countertop. The barman snatched the notes without looking and nodded at the next customer to call out their order. The large metal door clicked when the bouncer saw me approaching, then jolted slightly. I pushed it open with my elbow, squeezed through the opening and heard the locking mechanism snap shut behind me.

I found myself trapped in a halo of blinding light. Looking up at the powerful outside lamps, I almost sensed the light burn through the corneal surface of my eyes. I have no doubt that the light was a deterrent for weekend pub brawls, or to assist the cops when responding to a fight, or rather, the paramedics when responding to a stab or gun wound.

The glare was made worse by the sudden arrival of mist, a result of the drop in temperature during the last hour, which had precipitated the sudden condensation. Another cold front was on the way. The mist had a dewy density to it and clung to my clothes. I shuddered as goosebumps crawled across my skin. I pulled the hoodie tight and stretched out my arms to counter the chill.

My eyes adjusted slowly. I looked left, then right, slowly panning the street and peering into the dark nooks of shopfronts, alleyways, and staircases. I thought I had lost them, then made out the three shapes getting into a nondescript car off to my right. I got into my little Honda, very nonchalantly, and tailed them towards the edge of town where Kraaifontein merged with Brackenfell. I kept a safe following distance, at times dimming the Honda's headlights to remain inconspicuous. Whenever the car in front of me slowed, its rear red lights flared up, then I followed suit. Their car turned left, heading to the Stellenbosch winelands. Soon after, it turned left once more onto a deserted road.

Tall buildings became trees, then a flatter terrain. The town and its lights drifted away until it was a small square in my rear-view mirror. The mist grew thicker still, and the darkness became impenetrable. As I grew wary of their level of incognizance about the Honda behind them, I turned my headlights to dim and drove on in darkness. It was not nearly as harrowing as I imagined. At times I heard the crunch of gravel under the tires when I drifted onto the shoulder of the road.

The red lights flared again as the car drew to a halt, then the lights went out. I pulled up onto the side of the road, the steering wheel vibrating in my hands as the car idled, then I drove further into the field until the car was concealed by shrubs. I killed the engine, put off the roof light and got out of the car as quietly as I could. I recalled where I had last seen the red lights but couldn't make out anything else. The mist was incredibly dense. I wavered for about a minute to take in my surroundings.

I was standing in a patch with knee-high wild grass. It brought back the memory of the long grass at the glass factory. In the distance I made out a couple of shapes that could be buildings. I had passed a familiar lot with rentable storage units earlier, so I had a rough idea where I was. By my estimation, there were a couple of decent wine farms not too far from there. The smell of cow dung or compost lingered in the air, reminded me of farmlands.

In the distance I heard a soft scraping sound, like that of a large piece of metal scraping against another piece of metal. I was quite far away from the sound.

As I pushed through to the edge of the road, the dew from the grass was transferred to my sneakers. By the time I got to the tarred surface, my shoes and socks were soaked through. I hunched over and walked along the tarred road, closing the gap between myself and the stationary car. Three minutes later, the road turned into a fine gravel. I moved back to the shoulder of the road, where I walked along a sandy strip until a large building quickly came into view. It appeared right in front of me, as though the mist had kept it hidden until I was about to bump into it. Then I heard someone's laughter ripple through the quiet night. It was very close. A couple of meters away.

I froze.

Thankfully my jacket and hoodie were light grey and my jeans and sneakers were faded blue. If I did not move, I would be imperceptible until someone bumped into me. At that point, hearing the light scrunch of feet and a strained cough in front of me, I regretted not bringing Gavin's gun with me.

A car's boot slammed shut and then the sounds died down as the three men trudged off to one side. They slipped into what seemed like the mouth of a narrow passageway between two buildings. Their voices echoed slightly from the bottom of the confined space.

I went to the mouth of the alley, nearly walking into the wall of the other building. I slipped into the alley and moved towards the voices. Every time I placed my next step, I rolled my sneaker from heel to toe, taking care not to betray my presence. I wiped at the condensation that had formed around my nostrils to avoid a surprise sneeze. I was moving forward slowly, pushing through the mist, hunched over, hugging the wall, when a large, dark shape came into view in front of me. I stopped and inspected it with one hand. The surface of the obstruction was cold and hard to the touch. Underneath my fingertips, I felt the tiny bubbles of rust under a painted metal surface. I waved at the grey mist to clear the droplets and saw faint yellow letters spelling: SKIP.

I leaned back and looked up at a large open-topped, trapezium-shaped waste container resembling the dumpster receptacles often found on construction sites. I realized that there was a row of large skip containers lining the wall to the left. Due to its shape, there was a space between the wall and the base of each skip. With all the skips lined up, it created a man-sized wormhole. Without applying any rational thought, I went down on my hands and knees and crawled into the triangular tunnel.

The thought of me dirtying my clothes or crawling in a space where rats and other nocturnal critters roamed for food was completely overruled by the notion that I had nothing left to lose. I was a dead man crawling. If I snagged my leg on a rusty nail and died of tetanus, it would be no worse than dying of brain cancer in the coming months, weeks, or days.

I shuffled along as quietly as possible, lifting my leg each time to avoid making unnecessary sounds. With every knee shuffle, the voices grew louder.

"Is that the last of the dope," Dumeko said from the bottom of the alley.

"I can't see shit down here, man," said Errol.

I heard feet move about, some grunts, then the sound of a duffel bag being zipped shut.

"I guess that's all of it."

"Why are we moving the whole load?" Lloyd said in a tense whisper. "We just moved it here last month."

There was a long pause where no one said anything, then Dumeko spoke up.

"The boss says we move it, so we move it."

The wind spiralled down the wormhole and clung to my body, adding weight to my clothes. The stench of urine was overwhelming, as was the dark pressing in on me. The only thing that kept me going was the triangle of dense white mist at the end of the tunnel.

Finally, I came to the fifth and final skip receptacle. My breathing was harsh from the exertion. Sweat was streaming down my face and my lips were dry. I sensed a spell coming but urged it back. I rested against the wall for support and willed the dizziness away.

Outside the tunnel, I heard a door swinging on hinges and then being slammed shut. After a while, I heard scuffling and slapping sounds as if someone returned from the car at the bottom of the alley.

"Hey, what are you doing?" Lloyd said.

"Chill, bro," said Errol. "You going to stay here. Keep watch over this place for us."

I slowly pushed my head all the way out from the crawlspace to get a better view. Through the mist I was barely able to see Errol and Dumeko prodding Lloyd with their hands. Lloyd protested, but Dumeko motioned him to stand still, then slowly raised a finger to his lips and shushed him. The coldness in his eyes was so menacing that it cautioned me to stop fidgeting in my tunnel.

"What's going on?" Lloyd asked after a while.

Errol nodded when he was satisfied that he had inspected Lloyd's body thoroughly, then Dumeko stepped back and stared at Lloyd for a long time.

"What?" said Lloyd.

"No wire?"

"What?" Lloyd repeated, but this time his voice faltered.

"We know you are meeting with the cops, bro. We've been watching."

Lloyd tensed up and began shifting around. He raised his hands, slowly shook his head, licked his lips and attempted to explain, everything a guilty person would do once found to be guilty.

"*Ubuqili wena*," Dumeko grunted in Zulu as he pulled a gun from his waistband. "I respect that, but in this business snitches don't run far."

I was still trying to catch up with events when the gun went off. *Bam!* It was fast and loud, blaring and reverberating in the confines of the alley. The muzzle flash was a burnt orange spark trapped in the thick mist. Lloyd's head rocked back, a faint cloud of red hanging on the mist as his body went limp. He slumped to the ground in a heap, as though his body had disappeared and only his clothes had been left behind.

I didn't dare to blink. My thoughts stalled and my muscles tightened. The dizzy spell I had felt coming seconds ago crawled back into hiding. The scorched smell of gunfire wafted down to where I lay. That somehow made it even more real.

"*Uxolo, bra* Lloyd," whispered Dumeko.

Errol took up Lloyd's arms. Dumeko tested the temperature of the gun's barrel, waved it about a couple of times, then slipped it back into the waistband of his chinos. He took Lloyd's feet and helped Errol to move the body further back into the dark alley.

At that point I felt a tickling sensation as something scampered across my legs. Tiny claws or teeth poked through my socks where the cuffs of my jeans had pulled away. I lifted my leg and kicked at the air until it let go of my leg. Whatever it was, it fell to the ground with a soft thud and ran towards my head, exiting the tunnel ahead of me. I saw a brownish, hairy smudge zip across my line of sight, then heard a soft squeak and a rattle as the critter disappeared into a pile of garbage. When I shifted my eyes back to Dumeko, he was looking right at me. He was still holding Lloyd's legs, but his eyes were focused intently on the section where the skip and the wall formed a dark triangle, where the sound had originated from.

I didn't breathe. I had no idea whether he had seen me, or whether he imagined there was an outline of a hoodie. All I knew was that my head was fully protruding from the tunnel. If he hadn't seen me yet, he would certainly see me if I made the slightest move. So, I waited.

"Come on, man," Errol complained. "The dude is getting heavy."

Dumeko slowly turned back to Errol and began shifting Lloyd's body.

I let out the air inside my lungs and breathed a soft sigh of relief.

"So, we just going to leave him here?"

"Yea, this place is burned. It belonged to one of the farmers here, but the Government bought the whole property a couple months ago, skips and all. They want to put up a community centre here."

"A community centre? Out here?"

"Exactly. They won't find his body until next year. By then they won't even know who it belongs to. The rats will clean him off for us. And if they find him sooner then it's just a message to the coppers of what we do to snitches."

When they were satisfied, Dumeko kicked Lloyd's one boot and studied the body for a reaction.

"Nah, he's dead, bro," said Errol.

"Come, we still need to drop the dope."

"At the new spot? Next to the bakery?"

"Yea, Denvor's getting paranoid. The auto shop will double as our dumpsite. It looks clean. No more moving shit around."

"I need to stop for smokes, bro."

"No more stoppages," Dumeko said and removed a pack of cigarettes from a back pocket. "Here, take mine."

The two men left. The red brake lights cast an ominous red glow into the alley when the car engine fired up, then I heard the tires crunch over the gravel as it rolled into the night. The crunching sound grew faint, then an unbearable silence took hold of the night. I lay there for a minute or two, then crawled out of my hiding spot.

My clothes were dirty, so I brushed my hand over my pants and jacket. I trembled all over, probably because of the excitement of not having been noticed.

My aim in coming there was to find out where Denvor stored his drugs. When following him around, I recalled his visit to a family bakery in an industrial area. It had been quite recently. There were leasing signs with red lettering displayed in the building's windows. I reasoned that if that was the new location where Denvor stored his drugs, then I could take some pictures and feed that information to the police.

I was still chewing on the new information when there was a gurgling cough behind me.

CHAPTER 22

Through the dense mist, I made out Lloyd's body crumpled up in a far corner. I stared at his worn-out brown boots. No movement. I stepped out from behind the cover of the large metal container and peered into the white haze towards the end of the alley. Nothing.

I was about to leave when there was another cough.

Again, I turned towards the back of the alley. I focused intently on Lloyd's body, my breath caught. I waited like that for a long time, anxious and taut, unsure whether there was someone else in the alley or whether my mind was playing tricks on me again.

There was another cough. This time it startled me. My nerves snapped and my chest tightened. At least this time I discerned a shift through the mist where Lloyd's head was. I moved a bit closer to his body and waved cautiously at the mist to improve visibility. The tiny droplets dragged sideways in the wake of my hand.

When Lloyd coughed again, his head lolled sideways.

I shuffled towards the enclosed section at the back of the

alley. I lead with my left shoulder, my right hand bunched into a fist, ready to swing if Dumeko or Errol lunged at me from the impenetrable white haze.

When I reached Lloyd, I edged around to his right side. My back brushed against a wire mesh fence as I hunched down. I was bent over him, lowering my head to get a better look. All was fine and well until his face appeared through the mist. There was a round hole in the centre of Lloyd's forehead where the projectile had punched through his skeleton, with a smudge of red around it. However, his left cheek was blotted blue and horribly swollen, his left eye was partially bloodshot, and a tiny trail of blood led out of his left ear. There were no messy exit wound or bits of brain to be seen. Just a disfigured face wearing the mask of death. I imagined that the bullet must have ricocheted off the back of Lloyd's skeleton and mushroomed or lodged somewhere inside the left side of his head.

At that point his right eye shifted sideways and focused on me. It blinked slowly, with effort. I felt a hand wrap around my ankle and bunch into a tight grip. It was the same ankle a rodent had scampered across earlier, and the same hand that, moments before, had pleaded its innocence.

I jumped up, pulled my leg free, and fell back against the wire fence, bouncing to one side and crashing into a couple of old crates. The wood shattered underneath my weight, a large splinter piercing through my jeans and into my one butt cheek. I sat up and stared at Lloyd in disbelief.

There was another strained cough. Then he swung his right hand up and down, looking for my ankle. He coughed again, and again, until a wash of blood dribbled out of his mouth and splattered over his shirt. While the mist muted all other colours, the dark red blood seemed to penetrate the dense condensation, as though the life inside of it was calling out for help. I got up and leaned over him again. His bloodied lips moved up and down, forming words. I strained to listen but couldn't make out what he was trying to say. It sounded like he was saying *cosa… cosa…*, but he kept trailing off, wavering at the very edge of death. He appeared to muster up a last bit of energy, forcing his lips to cooperate. The three words that came out made no sense at all. They were spread across three quick, panicked breaths. *All … ectif … cosa.*

After Lloyd had uttered those three words, the most profound breath escaped from the inner parts of his soul, snuck out of his lungs, up his windpipe and blew out through his open mouth in a long, ghostly sigh. The pained expression on his face became contorted for a second or two, then relaxed. His one eye gradually became distant, and the eyelids fully parted in death.

A cold chill crept up my spine. I rose to my feet. Instantly tiny spots flared up across my periphery, which caused an attack of vertigo, made worse by the density of the mist. I leaned back against the fence and hooked my fingers on the mesh to remain standing. I took in the eerie silence and focused on the steady sound of my breathing. This had worked on another occasion.

The oncoming attack halted when I heard a rustling sound near the mouth of the alley, followed by the faintest whisper of footsteps approaching. It was impossible to see anything through the mist, but I could hear someone coming down the alley. The vertigo subsided in waves as I slid down the fence. I went onto my hands and knees and crawled towards the back of the waste receptacle, hoping to make it to the tunnel before the mystery guest arrived. But I was too late.

Before I could reach the metal skip, I found myself staring down at the tips of a pair of brown leather lace-up shoes. The left shoe tip shifted back, as if in recognition of my presence, then settled in an awkward stance.

There was a buzzing sound in my head, much like the amplified sound of blood rushing in my ears. Bits of gravel and tar pressed into my hands. With my hoodie pulled askew and half of my face exposed, my cheeks had gone numb. Because of the damp that clung to my clothes, exacerbated by the familiar Cape Town breeze that zephyred down the alley, I was cold to my bones. Yet despite this, an inexplicable warmth had rushed up to my head.

I leaned back slowly, raising my hands as though someone with a gun had told me to surrender. I tipped all the way back until I rested on my haunches, then I looked up at Bertie September.

We were both trapped in this tense moment that felt longer than what it really was, best defined by the quantum physics term called superposition, stuck in a decision-making paradigm, a limbo before reaching a decision.

Bertie looked confused. His tiny brows were scrunched up and his eyes were narrowed slits. He was taking in what he was seeing, but I could tell that his mind was struggling to digest it. His gaze rested on the dead body for a long time, blood still clearly visible over Lloyd's jacket, then panned down to where I was.

Again, his gaze shifted to Lloyd's body, then back until our eyes met once more.

"It's not what you think," I heard myself say in a weird, gravelly voice.

Bertie looked incredibly vexed. Alarm was painted all over his features. He began shaking his head, then took a quick step back, shaking his head faster.

"No, wait. Let's talk…" I began, but I could tell he had reached the point where fight-or-flight had become flight.

He took another step backward and was about to turn and run back from where he had come. Without thinking about the consequences, I leapt to my feet and went after him. He was surprisingly fast. It took me a couple of steps to catch up with him. He was just beyond my reach, with the mouth of the alleyway beckoning, so I did something ungentlemanly. My fingers caught hold of his fleece jacket's hoodie. I stopped dead and jerked the hoodie back, pulling Bertie clean off his feet. My sudden strength surprised me.

Bertie tumbled backward, clumsily bumping into my legs and knocking me down on top of him. I put out a hand to stop my fall as I continued to roll over him, but my head bounced off the edge of one receptacle with a loud, buzzing *clang*. My entire world shook, with a sudden splatter of twinkling white spots playing across the grey mist.

I gripped in the haze until my fingers dug into clothing. I used my weight to keep Bertie from getting up. He was writhing and kicking, his hands pushing into my chest, swinging at my head but glancing off to one side.

"You sick son of a bitch," he screamed. "You've gone too far."

Before I could stop it from happening, the fingers of both my hands were clasped around his neck. They squeezed involuntarily, tightening, turning, as though trying to open a large jar of pickles. I had no control. My hands and fingers were doing things that I had not told them to do. And it felt good.

Bertie's screaming stopped dead in his throat, his eyes tensed and widened, and his breathing became hoarse. I felt his blood pulse through one throbbing vein on the side of his neck. He clawed at my hands, but his efforts were feeble. I pushed down on his throat, hard, sure that he was within seconds from dying at my hands.

A sudden sharp pain flashed through my head. My eyesight went completely blank, and my entire body went limp. I fell over on top of Bertie and blacked out for a couple of seconds.

It must have been mere seconds, because when I came to, Bertie was pushing my body off his and struggling to his feet, coughing and wheezing as he steadied himself against a large waste bin. My eyesight had returned but the white spots were still jumping around.

Bertie staggered over me and headed towards the end of the alley. He faded into the mist and then he was gone. I made no effort to pursue him. I was incapacitated. I had no fight left in me. Whatever energy had been there before had been snatched from my reserves. The more I tried to roll over, the more I became aware of my inability to do so. The slightest movement caused my head to ache.

The cold air fell over me and became firmer with each passing minute, until it felt as if I was trapped in a coffin. I have no idea how long I rested there, but it had to be about half an hour or more. Eventually I rolled over onto my side and pushed my body up. I was tingling and shaking all over. I felt my way out of the alley, moving slowly and carefully until I felt sure my legs could carry my body again.

As my sneakers crunched across the gravel, Lloyd's last words kept repeating in my mind. *All ... ectif ... cosa.* By the time I reached my little Honda, most of my energy had returned to me, though something inside my head was off, out of sorts. The debilitating episode that came over me while I was strangling Bertie had left me fragile for a long time after. Whoever I had been when I entered that alley, I was not the same person when I stumbled out of it.

The Honda crawled out from its hiding place, mounted the edge of the road and slipped into the mist as though it had never been there.

CHAPTER 23

It took me a couple of weeks to come to terms with what had happened in the alley. Lloyd's lifeless face haunted me for the first two nights, then I gradually became numb to the memory of it. There was a momentary concern that the incident had rendered me remorseless, but the thought dissipated when Brenda's gentle face flashed inside my mind.

The contrasting images of Brenda smiling and kissing my hand, and that of Lloyd's sightless, bloodshot eye, caused me to contemplate my own death with a sense of clarity. My death was not only imminent, according to my doctor, it was almost overdue. He said I was living on borrowed time. Once that reality took up residency in my mind, ambivalence became a luxury I could ill afford.

Initially, I was concerned that Bertie would report the incident and finger me for Lloyd's murder, but it dawned on me that I had already paid him a handsome sum of money. His hands were now as dirty as mine. In some sick way, he was an accomplice in all of this, my dance partner, the second ox bearing the weight of the yoke. Any attempt to implicate me in a crime would only implicate himself.

As I revisited the incident in my mind, I became more concerned that a small army of police officers would be on my trail. I was no crime scene investigator, but I'd watched enough shows to know that I had left some form of physical evidence in the alley. The large wooden splinter of the shattered crate had pierced into my buttocks and left quite a scar. That splinter surely had some of my blood on it. Also, when I banged my head against the waste bin, it had torn the skin open across my forehead. That would be some solid DNA evidence to chase up.

My fears served little purpose because nothing ever happened. Lloyd's body was never discovered. Or, rather, it was never reported anywhere. As the gang war between Denvor and Shane raged on, I listened to the news daily but never heard anything about a body being discovered in an alley. This provided some insight into Lloyd's parting words. *All ... ectif ... cosa.*

Those words had stumped me, but the answer came to me one evening when I returned from my radiation therapy. I drove by a police station and saw the blue light underneath the SAPS insignia. The unforgettable image of Detective Xhosa sucking on his cigarette flashed inside my mind, which instantly led me to think that Lloyd had asked me to *"call Detective Xhosa."* The realization that this could have been Lloyd's last words, meant that he had probably been Xhosa's informant, which further explained Dumeko's comments before shooting Lloyd. I wasn't sure what to do with that information. I knew calling Detective Xhosa would make no difference at all; it might even make my situation worse. I didn't fancy the idea of spending my last days in a jail cell while awaiting court hearings.

A couple of weeks passed. My window of opportunity was

narrowing, not only because of my illness, but also because of the escalation of the turf war. The battle between Collins and Daniels was burning white hot. There were newspaper headlines about incidents where people were gunned down in the streets. Foot soldiers, drug dealers and innocent people were all falling victim to this feud. What made matters worse was the vigilante-style killing of Macky Collins, Shane's crazy half-brother. It happened during a two-day period when I was exceptionally ill after my therapy treatments. I had to forego my investigative efforts while recuperating, but the team of private investigators on my payroll had things covered. Apparently, Macky had been shot five times, then dumped in a maintenance pit at an abandoned glass factory. Police had discovered the body a week after his disappearance. They also found the body of Gavin Snyders, a contract killer rumoured to have ties with major operators in the southern suburbs. Macky's body had to have been dumped into the pit long after I had rolled Gavin's body into it, but at least a week before one of my investigators had made an anonymous call to the police. It was eerie that Gavin had never been reported missing. He had no family and no friends.

Two of my personal investigators said they could no longer spend time on the Collins-Daniels investigation because it was getting too dangerous and they feared for their lives. The other investigators followed suit soon after. Collins blamed Daniels for Macky's killing, and Daniels blamed the dealers from the southern suburbs, whom Macky had often aggravated by means of his scandalous adventures in Goodwood. The situation was getting out of control. I had to remind myself that I wanted to stop the slaughter of the innocents, which was the only casualty worthy of mention at this point. Instead, it was getting worse for everyone.

My illness was also advancing. For a short while, minor improvements had me entangled in a net of hope. When the cancer retaliated, Andre told me that the red X on my calendar was unlikely to be pushed back again. He surmised that I had, at best, a month or two left, which didn't sit well with me. I explained that I was feeling much better and that the scans had to be wrong, to which Andre only said that things would get better before they got worse.

He was right, of course. While my strength was returning to me, my sanity was departing from me. I saw shadows where there were none. The white spots had gone grey. My behaviour was erratic. There were moments of hilarity juxtaposed by bouts of sadness that left me heaving in bed until I passed out. I found myself doing things I would never have done before, like the day I snapped out of a spell in a clothing store, only to find myself urinating against a towel display rack in the homeware section. I remember the look of repulsion and shock on the fitting room attendant's face. Luckily, the manager on duty was aware of my condition. That, however, didn't make the memory any less humiliating when it returned to me. Try as I might, I could not remember how I had got to be in that store at that time. I mostly shopped online and hardly left the house to do shopping. There were other times where I wandered about or came to after a spell. For instance, I would think about the smell of coffee, then the next thing I would sit with a cup of coffee in front of me, as though I was merging the instigating thought with the enacting thereof for my own convenience. During spells, my aggression would only be directed at myself, though when I was of sound mind my focus was still to avenge those who had wronged me. I had to remove all the mirrors in my house, because I kept shattering them in absentia. Things were heading towards a pinnacle, though the pinnacle itself was still a mystery to me. Time became inconsistent. The anniversary of Brenda's death had come and gone, though I couldn't recall when or if it had affected me. What did affect me, though, was the sight of Brenda in a picture frame. All the confusion dissipated when she popped up in my mind, but it was followed by prolonged bouts of sadness.

My investigation had reached a point where it could not progress any further. I had accumulated the information I required, but my mind was struggling to digest it all. Moments of poor reasoning were sporadic, usually followed by moments of exceptional clarity. I took advantage of these moments to assemble the plan I had in store for the two criminals who had ruined my life.

It all came to a head one day as I sat at my desk and examined the extent of my work. Besides the office desk, which had belonged to my father, a small filing cabinet and my leather satchel, the room was void of furniture. In front of the desk, spread out neatly across the tiled surface of the floor, was all the information I had gathered over the last year. Files had been separated into groups, while the files in each group had been arranged according to thickness. The group relative to Shane Collins consisted of yellow files and the group relative to Daniels were red. Within these groups resided the full weight of my knowledge about Collins and Daniels, as well as the ten generals who did their dirty work.

Near the door was a group of green files which contained my

research on all the foot soldiers, drug dealers, prostitutes, club owners and other tradesmen who had illicit dealings with either Collins or Daniels. I had compiled everything as actionable tip-offs that would hold great reward in the police's fight against gangsterism and drugs in the northern suburbs. I had made copies of the contents of the green files and had arranged for them to be delivered to Detective Xhosa following my death. He could pursue those culprits at will, though I suspected that any vacuum created in the northern suburbs drug world would only be filled by southern suburbs operators.

I gave myself one week to conclude my business.

I struggled to my feet and shuffled around the desk. I'd lost a lot of weight, but I still felt better than I had the month before. I made my way through the room, passing the groups of red, yellow and green files. I stopped near the door and stared at a smaller stack of files which had been isolated in an empty corner. The files were such a dark shade of blue that the black names written on them were almost indiscernible. The topmost file read: JAYDEN.

CHAPTER 24

In relocating to Camps Bay, I had set free most of the mementos that reminded me of Brenda and the life we had shared. I had scaled down tremendously. The apartment I had bought was purposely small and it required little maintenance. It was on the first floor of an exclusive complex that overlooked the beach. It was the breadth of my happiness.

I left my office and went to the living room. It was a large open room that merged with an open-plan kitchenette. I kept the coffee table and large flat screen TV. I purchased new couches because, during one of my spells, I had tried to cut out the dirt stains from my old couches with a pair of pliers. It was irreparable.

I had little to no use for kitchen items, so I gave everything away to the movers who had brought over my bed, refrigerator and coffee table. At that stage I lived on ready-made TV dinners. They were especially prepared for cancer patients and supplied by a local company on a weekly basis. It was like eating lasagna with all possible traces of lasagna removed from the dish. It was cancer-friendly mush.

I stepped through the empty, white living room. The silence was comforting. The sliding door pulled back with little effort. I stepped out into the cold sea breeze. The hair on my arms stood alert and my arms began to shiver. The salt of the sea rested inside my nostrils like a pleasant memory. From my balcony, I heard the early evening traffic whispering across the tarred roads. Further away, I made out the sounds of laughter and happiness sailing up from the beach. I closed my eyes and allowed my soul to take flight. Beyond the beach, I heard the shifting sea splash back on itself, the gentle push of the water rustling against the waves, causing the surf to froth so loudly that it crackled in my ears.

The worth of my life had come under scrutiny after my arrival in Camps Bay. I'd been so preoccupied with planning my revenge that I had sabotaged myself with anger and hate. Those emotions had partially consumed one part of me. However, everything had changed the day I met Jayden. It had been around the time that I was moving from our house to my little bachelor pad overlooking the beach. The movers had just finished unpacking my furniture. I had to rush to the clinic not to miss my treatment.

When I arrived at the clinic, they ushered me into a room. I wore my usual jeans and sneakers with the clinic's green frock pulled over my T-shirt. I remember the intoxicating smell of alcohol-based hand sanitizer as though it was still in my nose. They sat me beside a young boy and hooked me up to an IV station.

Jayden was about ten years old. He had a puffy face, high cheek bones and friendly eyes. He kept his arms crossed high up over his chest to keep from pushing against the connector of the IV system. When he saw me, his face lit up and a smile spread across his cheeks.

At the time, in between a series of intense treatments, his joy was a massive burden for me. Patients receiving treatment at clinics often had little to no motivation to remain positive, while others were so focused on faking their personal happiness that it was agonizing to watch them wither away with a desperate smile on their face. I believed that any attempt at happiness while receiving chemoradiotherapy would be staying in denial.

I sensed no objection in Jayden's demeanour, though. He was jovial because he chose to be. He was not new to treatment, either. I had seen him there before that day. Though not terminal, he had been diagnosed with stage 4 Hodgkin's lymphoma. He had been fighting cancer far longer than I had, but his was a fight worth rooting for.

"Hello, Mister," he said when the nurse left the room.

"Hey," I greeted, then I pointed at the machines. "It's not nice to see a young man like yourself hooked up to one of those things."

Jayden inspected the drip as though he had never noticed it before. He played with his tongue across the tips of his large teeth, then smiled again. He stared at me with his deep brown eyes. I had never experienced such an intense stare in all my life. It cut right through me.

"Do you think someone else would want to take my place?"

My attempt at a smile might have been the saddest thing the poor boy had ever seen.

"I didn't think so," he said, shrugged and curled up his lips in a playful manner. "I'll have to push through and get this over with then."

I was taken aback by his emotional maturity, his choice of

words and his playfulness.

"What's your name, son?"

"Jayden. What's yours?"

I looked around the room to see if there were other patients receiving treatment behind the partition screens. We were alone in the room, our machines beeping sporadically as it paced the intake of our medication. Without realizing it, my fingers were playing with the gray cancer ribbon I had pinned on my shirt.

"Gray," I answered.

"Mr. Gray?"

"No," I said absently as the ribbon became undone across my heart. "Just Gray, with an 'a', like the American spelling. No mister." I fumbled with the remains of the ribbon.

"What do you have?" he asked. My confused look caused him to point to the connector where the IV fed into my arm. "What type of cancer?"

"GBM," I said. "Glioblastoma multiforme."

He stared at me for a few seconds, then smiled again.

"Cool. That sounds way better than mine. Hodgkin's sounds like a pudding or porridge. Yours sound like a superhero identity, like a fake name that a hero would use when he's out saving lives or doing good."

There was a brief silence.

"How long do you have left?"

I suppressed an instinctive gasp. His question had been so direct that I couldn't retreat from it. I had no idea how to talk about diseases and mortality with a ten-year-old boy, especially not when it came to me unannounced.

"It's OK," he said. "I won't tell anyone."

I rubbed at my forehead, lost in thought, and fighting for my solemnity. He was tugging at the door to a room I had kept private for so long. Try as I could, I couldn't find a valid argument to keep this boy from seeing my misery and my confusion. He was the embodiment of innocence.

"I don't really know," I said finally, sighing as I set the words free from captivity. "Not long, I guess."

"See, that wasn't so hard."

"And you? How long do you have?"

"Me?" He sounded surprised. "Oh, no, I'm fighting this thing. I have my whole life ahead of me. I'm not going to let it beat me."

We continued in this way with a bizarre sagacious banter for the better part of an hour when an unhealthily thin nurse came in and detached his drip. He pulled off his green frock and rolled his shoulders over in annoyance. He looked on as the nurse detached my drip.

"You done?" Jayden asked, his voice was husky and warm.

"Not yet. I must go in there so the next lady can zap my brains."

His eyes grew wide in amazement. His forehead expanded so much that his curly hair pulled back in an obscure manner.

"What? For real?"

I nodded.

"That's so cool!"

He gave the nurse an intimidating stare, who offered him a wry smile in return. "Only zap the bad parts, Miss. This man needs his brain."

I followed Jayden out the door and into the corridor. The next part of my treatment would be done in the room across the way.

"Mommy!" he called and shot down the corridor.

My sneakers squeaked over the linoleum floor as I made my way towards the next room. The sound echoed down the narrow corridor and tugged at Jayden's curious sense of entertainment.

"Hey," I heard behind me. "Come meet this man, Mommy."

My body was already strained after the treatment. Or maybe the tumor in my brain was forcing out its apprehension of the coming radiotherapy. Either way, my body was fighting with my mind, and my spirit was caught in the middle. It was a futile bout, with no victor.

As my one hand curled around the cold steel door handle, I felt Jayden's soft warm hand taking hold of my other. The warmth of his body and his innocence nearly drove me to tears at that point. The closer I edged towards death, the more I treasured the life of others.

"Gray," he said. "This is my mom. Mom, this is Gray."

She was a small woman. The intensity of her spirit leapt out at me when her almond eyes locked with mine. Her smile was forced, but I could sense a sincerity inside of her that could not be detained. It radiated outward and bounced off the walls of the corridor. I instantly liked her.

"Good to meet you," she said, without offering her name in return. She touched her braided hair self-consciously, gently pulling Jayden back as only a protective mother could.

I greeted, smiled, and let go of Jayden's hand. I did not let go of the door handle.

I realized two things at that moment. The first was that Jayden's mother was his inspiration and his source of positivity. Of that, I had no doubt. The other thing was that I had seen this woman before. She showed no sign of recognizing me, but I was convinced I had seen her before.

"We have to go, baby," she said in a firm tone.

"Pleased to have met you, Jayden's Mom," I said in my most sociable tone, then to Jayden, "You keep on fighting, young man."

We parted ways. His jovial chatter carried down the corridor as the door pulled shut behind me. I replayed the encounter throughout my radiation session, then went home.

Jayden and I were chemo buddies a couple of times after that. He told me about his mother and his grandparents, how they played with their dog in the park, took turns throwing balls, and dug out sea snails when visiting the beach. He was a bright boy, and his positivity was infectious. I traversed the plains of my memory in search of Jayden's mother but could not find any sign of her. My memory-filing glitch was unpredictable. I could access some memories at will, while others shifted around in the shadows. Regardless, my brain was telling me that I should have known this woman.

The sound of the sea brought me back to my balcony. I opened my eyes and stared out over the large expanse of water that stretched out in front of me. Its endlessness drew me into a moment of peace, then slowly released me back into the world. I went back inside and slid the door shut behind me. I prepared a cup of herbal tea and plonked down on the couch.

One morning not too long ago, Jayden had received his final treatment. He was in remission. He was winning his fight.

"Mom says we're going to kick cancer's butt," he had said.

I had returned from my treatment incredibly vexed. For the first time since our time together, Jayden had mentioned his father. The absence of a father had never concerned me, but when he spoke about a custody battle between his mother and his father, it had perked my interest. After I asked, he reluctantly gave me his father's name. The revelation was nothing extraordinary, but it was enough to persuade me that even the slightest coincidence had merit of influence.

When the nurse returned, I asked her to take a photo of the two of us hooked up to the IV systems, green frocks and nervous smiles. I waited for him to finish his treatment, cut mine short and left. I raced home and went into my study where I searched through the red files in the Denvor Daniels stack of files. I took out the file of Vuyo Jola and paged through the contents until I found a photograph of a woman in a pantsuit. In the picture, the woman was walking out of the Bellville Magistrates' Court building, one hand pressing a cellular phone to her ear and the other holding Jayden's hand. His face had been turned away when the private investigator took the shot. Without seeing his smile or his bright eyes, I could tell it was Jayden. Vuyo Jola and Sindi Makwetu had been engaged in a tense custody battle over their son. Vuyo had tried furiously to win, but his arrest record and his involvement with drug dealers had caused favor to rest with the only sense of security in Jayden's life, his mother. Because the child had been born out of wedlock, the name and surname of Vuyo and Sindi's only child was listed as Simphiwe Jayden Makwetu in the legal documentation.

I had printed out the photo the nurse had taken of us at the clinic, added it to a pile of documents, then slipped the paperwork into a blue file and wrote his name on it in capital letters. That had signalled the end to my research. Jayden had been the final piece missing from my elaborate puzzle. After adding his file to the months of research, an inexplicable calm came over me. I immediately went on to the next phase, bringing me back to the empty apartment and the warm cup of herbal tea.

I finished my tea and took in the quietude. The wind outside had started up as though announcing the arrival of a storm. I shivered. I was about to get dressed for the night when the doorbell rang.

No one knew where I lived. No one cared. Or so I thought.

I put my cup in the washbasin and peered into the peephole to see who my visitor was. I sighed and rested my forehead against the door.

"I know you are in there," the annoying voice said.

I pulled the door back and left it ajar. I returned to the comfort of the couch. There I waited until the door closed. Bertie September slunk into the living room as though he was walking on air. In one hand he held his leather satchel, with the other he pushed his spectacles back until it pressed into the bridge of his nose. He gave me a cheery half-salute.

It was the first time I had seen him since our altercation in the alleyway. For the briefest period, I thought I had seen the last of Bertie. Some part of me should have known he would come back into my life.

He rolled his eyes around the apartment. My bedroom was off to one side and my study was off to the other. An en-suite bathroom adjoined the bedroom. It smelled of vomit and detergent. The bedroom smelled of deathly sleep, the office of determination and the kitchen of herbal tea infusions.

"Spiffy place," he said in his whiny voice. "Smaller than I thought."

"I thought we had concluded our business. I paid you to leave me alone."

He went to the opposite couch and wiped it with a napkin

before sitting down. The couch was still brand new. No one had ever sat in it.

"Paid *me*?" he asked in surprise. "That was just a down payment. I also think you owe me something for trying to kill me."

"Oh, would you just piss off. You're not getting another cent from me, pal. I told you to leave me alone the last time and you almost paid the price for not listening."

He opened his satchel and removed a page. He scanned through it and folded it over. Bertie slid the page across the table, licking his lips as he did it. For some reason I thought back to the day my father slid a missing page from my homework assignment across the table during breakfast, his cunning and thoughtful manner not dissimilar as that of Bertie.

"I'm not doing this again," I said and got up from the couch. "You know the way out."

I got dressed and prepared myself for the night ahead as though I was alone in the apartment. Bertie was there, but to me he also wasn't there. I couldn't care in the least what he was up to. I had no interest in engaging with the man beyond what I already had.

He sat quietly in the living room and waited for me to finish. His small hands were crossed over his crotch. He pouted his lips as he stared out the sliding doors, taking in the sight as though it calmed him.

When I returned, I was clad in black cargo pants and a matching sweater, cheap knock-off combat gear purchased at a Chinese imports shop. I swallowed a load of vitamin boosters in the hope that it would energize me sufficiently. Tonight, I was going to kill Denvor Daniels.

"Thought I told you to leave?" I said softly.

He leaned forward, peering up at me over the rims of his spectacles and tapped a finger on the folded page.

"We need to talk about this first." This sounded eerily similar to what my dad had told me.

"I said no."

When I slumped into the couch, Bertie sat back so that I was forced to look at him. His eyes bore into me from across the room and kicked down the door I had been guarding. It was as though he knew where I kept my secrets and had the key to unlock them at will.

"We need to look at these payments. It is time."

"You are not a claims investigator, are you?"

"Heavens, no." Bertie giggled, more to himself than in response to my question. "Whatever gave you that idea?"

"You did. When you first introduced yourself. You said so."

"Did I really say that? Are you sure?"

Bertie got up and went into the kitchen. He removed a cup and a spoon as though he had watched me do it a hundred times before, as though this was his apartment, and I was paying him a visit.

"It doesn't sound like something I'd say."

He made us herbal tea while I slipped on my new boots. I was dreading the possibility of chafing my feet before the night was done. Even my loafers and my sneakers hurt my toes these days. A week ago, I had battled an infection on one toe. I had learned that, with my immune system in tatters, minor cuts and scrapes could become lethal if not dealt with promptly.

"Who are you working for?"

Bertie put the cup on the table, dipped one finger into his tea and licked it off. He sighed and leaned back into the couch as though a great pleasure washed over him.

"I work for whoever welcomes me through the door."

"What does that mean? You forced yourself into my business from the start."

"That's not true, is it? I only nibbled on what you fed me. Or, rather, you only nibbled on what I fed you. I'm not exactly sure which is which, or who is who."

"Rubbish, you were following me around all this time, looking for ways to get in on the action."

"I can understand that you think that, given your condition," he said. "Then again, all of us finance guys look the same, don't we?"

I stood up and left the room. I fetched Gavin's weapon from the bedroom cupboard and slipped it into one of the large side pockets of my pants. I put the silencer in the pocket on the other side.

Sensing that our meeting was at an end, Bertie rose and made his way to the doorway.

"You should know that I made anonymous calls to Daniels and Collins earlier," he said as an afterthought. "I painted them an embellished picture of who you are. Enough to make them think you are a drug supplier from Rondebosch muscling in on their territories. They sounded furious."

"Why the hell would you do that?" I screamed.

"I also called Xhosa and informed him about the location of Denvor's drug dump, as well as Shane's secret hideouts. It should hit the fan from tomorrow onwards."

"You are really messing up my plan," I said. "You understand what they did to me, to Brenda, to my family. Why do you do this now when I'm so close?"

Bertie licked his lips. He grimaced involuntarily, and said, "You are divided. Anger is muting the justice you are trying to claim. I've watched you plan your revenge, but you are going about it the wrong way. This will be better for everyone."

"Who are you to discredit my justice? Would you condemn me to justify yourself?"

He said nothing.

I dropped down on the couch. I was exasperated. My entire being was drained. It felt as though I was sparring with a prize fighter and coming up short.

"You aren't really Bertie September. Who the hell are you?" I asked in a defeated whisper. "What's your name?"

"You know who I am. Your memories are all jumbled up, but I'm in there. Look harder and you will find me." He gave me another half-salute and pointed at the page on the coffee table. "Make those payments. Time is running out. The fuse has been lit. They will come for you soon."

The door rattled shut behind him. His footsteps grew faint as he made his way down the walkway toward the entrance. I heard the gate whine open and slam shut as Bertie left the complex. A damning silence ensconced me in my little apartment and left me in a confused state. Night hastened after his visit. The golden dusk turned grey as shadows stretched across the world outside. I couldn't bring myself to look at Bertie's note. I left it on the table.

When sufficiently motivated, I snuck into the darkness, ready for malice. I promised myself that Denvor Daniels would not survive the night. He had to regret what he had done. He had to share in the pain he had inflicted on me. And then I would do the same to Shane Collins. To avenge Brenda.

What difference would it make if Bertie had indeed tipped them off? It would not alter my plans in the least. If anything, it would make them cautious.

CHAPTER 25

Denvor lived in a quiet neighbourhood on the outskirts of Kuils River. He was in the process of relocating to his new house in Highbury, which would be difficult to gain entry to because it was in a cul-de-sac in a new development with many open lots about. I had a narrow window of opportunity to take him out. The drive up from Camps Bay felt like an epic journey. My thoughts were in constant conflict. My mind kept wandering back to my meeting with Bertie. I had so many questions. This internal debate stirred up a headache.

I parked my Honda under a large tree a couple of blocks away. During my months of planning, this tree had always seemed like the safest spot to leave my car. I walked the rest of the way. It was early evening in the suburbs. The traffic was light. I kept to the shadows. Though cautious, I was fuelled by the notion that I was a dying man. Somehow that rendered the reality of death powerless. I was aware that the worst-case scenario would simply hasten death. With the end in sight, I didn't care if anyone saw me.

I had lost so much weight at this point that I must have looked like black smoke shifting across the tar, bouncing through the glare of the streetlamps. The soft grating sound of my laboured breathing echoed in my ears. The extreme exhaustion I had experienced early in my treatment had become familiar to me, so this was mild in comparison. My energy levels fluctuated haphazardly. At times I was dead tired, other times I was the best version of myself.

I rounded a corner and saw Denvor Daniels's double-story house take shape in front of me. It was a modest place for someone involved in the drug business. The house had a flat front façade, light grey with dark grey trim. I hadn't been inside yet, so I relied on pictures to gauge the dimensions and the layout of the house. There was a small balcony on the top floor where I assumed Denvor and his wife, Tamara, slept. I had numerous pictures of them sitting there in the mornings, engaged in deep conversation, sipping at cups while the steam blurred their faces. I suspected that the staircase leading up to this room would be at the back of the house, which was where I wanted to be.

In stark contrast, Shane Collins owned a mansion in Durbanville. He lived among the affluent and revelled in the joys that money wielded, much to the disdain of his neighbours. He had a horde of security on site, especially after his brother had been murdered. I was still not sure how I would kill Shane. Denvor was the easier target at this point.

During my reconnaissance, I noticed only two ways into the yard. Over the wall or through one of the gates. The main gate was a large black metal gate on a galvanized track at the bottom of a pebbled drive. Once the main gate was activated by remote, two lamps atop the side posts glared to life and the gate would roll open or shut. I had no remote and I wanted to avoid the light. The only other gate was a side gate to the right of the property, which led to a small porch and what was supposed to be the front door. This gate was obscured, seldom used and had a dated magnetic locking mechanism.

When I reached the barrier wall of the Daniels property, I hunched down in a nook behind a tree and slipped on the grey balaclava Gavin the hitman had bequeathed to me. My hair was starting to grow back after the chemo. That made my scalp itchy, but I suppressed the urge to scratch. Scratching led to tiny cuts, which led to infection, which I tried to avoid.

My research suggested that Denvor spent Wednesdays with his family. The security at his house was minimal, usually one guard in the front yard. His sleek black Jaguar sedan was nowhere to be seen. He usually arrived home around 8 PM or 9 PM, though this was never a set time. I looked at my watch. It was 7 PM. I had to get into the house before they returned.

I took out a small plastic bag from my backpack, which contained small pieces of raw sausage. At home, I had inserted veterinary-grade sedatives into the minced meat. I had inserted triple the required amount. I aimed and tossed it over the wall. From beyond the wall came a curious beastly growl, then I heard Denvor's two large Rottweilers rumbling and sniffing around in the grass, followed by the sound of jowls smacking.

The guard turned and approached the side gate. He was a stout man with a trimmed goatee. He wore a black sports jacket that fit so tightly that it made his arms flap in semicircles. He stopped at the gate and studied an approaching car. The beams of the car's headlamps poked into the darkness and swiped across the pavement where my feet were. I shifted my boots out of sight and hugged the tree. The guard sniffed, turned and waddled back towards the garage, his shoes crunching pebbles as he crossed the yard. He lit a cigarette, then kicked at the pebbles, which clinked as it ricocheted off the garage door.

Ten minutes passed and he didn't move. I was about to leave when an idea surfaced. I took out the weapon and screwed the silencer into the barrel. I worked slowly to avoid making a sound. The irony of working silently with a silencer was not lost on me. Once done, I steadied my body against the tree. The chips of tree bark were so hard that it bit into my shoulder. I had never used a weapon before, so I had no frame of reference. I was unsure what to expect. B-grade actioners with the likes of Van Damme or Seagal hadn't equipped me with weapons training. I recalled the cracking sound the weapon had made when Gavin had accidentally shot half his own face off. Not the most pleasant memory, but it gave me some idea of what to expect after I pulled the trigger. I extended my arm and pulled my head the other way, half-expecting the gun to explode in my hand. I closed one eye and aimed at a BMW parked on the opposite side of the road. I sucked in a slow, deep breath, then released it again. I gently squeezed the trigger at the same time that a car accelerated in the next block.

Nothing happened.

I stared at the gun in the glare of the streetlights, then remembered putting the safety catch on after the glass factory incident. I flicked the safety off, then took aim again. I waited for another audible distraction. In the distance I heard the rumble of a motorbike turning a corner, then it accelerated loudly, blaring down one of the backroads. I squeezed the trigger.

Almost all at once there was a muffled *crack*, then a puff of air, followed by a ripple that crept up my arms and into the base of my scalp. I heard a faint clunking sound as the bullet punched a hole somewhere on the car's metal body. Inadvertently I squeezed the trigger again when the motorcycle flew by behind me, its exhaust barking down the length of the street. I heard the welcoming crackle and smash of a side window. The car's alarm screamed into existence. The repetitive orange glow from the flicker units cast menacing shadows across the grey walls.

Using the sound of the alarm as a decoy, I mounted the side gate. I was halfway over when the main gate's lights flared up. The gate began rolling back on the track. If the guard had known where to look, he would have seen a black-clad figure perfectly poised on the top of the side gate. Instead, he stepped out into the road to see what the commotion was about.

I let go and fell to the ground on the inside of the property, losing my gun in the process. The spot where I landed was mostly covered with grass, though my upper body was subjected to the thorns of a rose bush. I extricated myself from the bushes as quietly as possible, lacerating my hands and cheeks in the process, again not considering the consequences of leaving DNA evidence behind. While the guard was distracted, I used the soft glow of the gate lights to locate the gun. Once reunited with my weapon, I crept across the front yard, passed the porch area, and hiked over another gate. The guard became engrossed in conversation with a neighbour. I used this opportunity to sneak around the side of the house.

I was about to try one of the side doors when I heard an obscene gurgling sound behind me. In my crouched position, I turned my upper body around very slowly, the heels of my boot grinding on the cement. I came face to face with one of Denvor's Rottweilers. Its head was tilted to one side, teeth bared. Its eyes were swimming around in its large skull as though it was unsure where to bite me. I raised the weapon and pointed it at the animal.

The strangest hesitation fell over me. I was there to murder a man, yet nothing inside of me was satisfied with the idea of killing his dog. While weighing up my options, the Rottweiler stepped this way and that, then tipped sideways and smacked into the wall. Its legs moved as though it was charging at me, but its eyes kept rolling over. A froth appeared in its jaws as it began biting at the air, then it yelped softly and dropped down again, this time motionless, falling victim to the tranquilizers I had fed it.

I didn't waste a second. I tried the door. It was locked. I moved around the backyard and found an open window through which my thin body would easily fit. On the grass I made out the shape of the second dog, sound asleep. I heard it snore as I shimmied through the narrow opening of the window. I tumbled onto a soft bed, bounced sideways and rolled across a carpet. I had to force my grunts into submission as I slammed into an empty laundry basket. I struggled to my feet.

I was in a bedroom that didn't see a lot of traffic. There were pillows arranged on the bed, but the curtains had been pulled shut and the bedside lamp had been unplugged. In one corner stood a couple of boxes partially filled with linen. The cupboard doors were ajar and had been emptied.

The corridor was deserted. There was a foyer section ahead of me. I saw no sign of a staircase to the left, so I figured that it had to be to the right. I prepared to make a run for it, but heard the guard clear his throat. I froze. My body tingled all over.

To the left, the garage doors rattled and banged. A stunning white light blazed to life. As the sound of a car's engine rumbled into the confines of the garage, the guard lumbered passed the room. He was so determined in his stride that he went by without looking my way. He crossed the foyer and went out to the front where he had previously been stationed, providing me with another opportunity to move further into the house. I flew down the corridor and up the steps. There were doors to two more rooms, but I went straight to the one I imagined would be Denvor's room, which was the big one with the balcony overlooking the front yard.

The room was dark, even though the dark grey curtains had been parted and slung over metal restraining hooks on either side. My eyesight was not what it used to be. I kept them focused on the light that played across the sheer curtains until my sight began to adjust. I eventually made out the bed, bedside cabinets, walk-in closet, vanity chest, a white cot for a baby and a large painting above the bed, which was warped by the shadows that divided the room. The shiny handles of the sliding door, leading onto the small balcony, were visible behind the sheer curtain.

I heard someone heading toward the stairway. The sound approached slowly, moving up the steps. I searched for a place to hide. The bed was too low for me to fit underneath. I inspected the en-suite bathroom off to the left, but there was no opportunity to hide myself. With white walls, white cupboards, and a white bath, there was no place to hide a black-clad Gray. The sound grew louder, footfalls of someone approaching. The person exited onto the landing and headed toward the room. In haste I opened the walk-in closet doors, stepped into the layers of clothing and closed it behind me. The wardrobe was smaller than I expected, but large enough for me to hide in. I raised the tip of the silencer and took aim through the slanted slats of the closet door as Tamara entered the room with a baby in her arms.

She was an attractive woman, with large eyelashes that I could make out even in the dark. The rest of her body moved across the shadows seductively, gracefully. She kicked off her shoes and turned towards the closet. I remembered studying her in the surveillance photos. She had a youthful appearance, shoulder-length brown hair and almond-coloured eyes. Her lips were thin and formed a resting half-pout. Her alluring qualities were drowned by a gentility that didn't fit the drug world. Though Denvor and Tamara had been together for years and were parents to a teenage daughter and a baby boy, I had no insight into the intricacies of their relationship. She stayed out of Denvor's affairs and tended to her children, but she still looked out of place, like a rose in the desert.

Tamara approached the walk-in closet. Her small feet sank into the thick carpet, emitting soft patting sounds that grew dangerously close. The floral qualities of her perfume drifted through the slats and pinned me deeper into the hanging clothes. My breath caught in my throat. I became one with the dresses and jackets that draped over my shoulders. Tamara stepped up to the cot, which stood right beside the closet doors and leaned into it with her upper body. She was so close to me that I could make out the strands of her hair in the dark, the curves of her breasts against her evening dress.

"There, there," Tamara whispered as she put her baby into the cot. She pulled the small blanket to one side and covered his tiny legs. When she was satisfied that the boy had gone back to sleep, she turned on her heel and left the room as swiftly and quietly as she had entered it.

I released a tense sigh and steadied myself against the inside wall of the closet to avoid passing out. I closed my eyes and rubbed my forehead as a wave of nausea hit me. My fingers trembled and my vision blurred. These bouts of sickness came quickly, but I had become attuned to its approach ever since the misty night I had witnessed Lloyd's murder.

I stepped out of the closet but nearly lost my balance. I gripped the side of the cot as the sickness washed over me, through me. I retreated into the closet space and waited there for about fifteen minutes as the spell dissipated. My vision went blank as the world disappeared. When I came to, I was hunched over next to the cot. My knuckles almost glowed white in the dark. I fought to regain control over my body. When I stood erect and let go of my grip, my hand burned from the pressure it had endured. I had no idea where I was or how I got there. When I noticed the weight of the gun in my hand, it jostled my memories. I remembered Bertie, sitting on the new couch in my apartment, his fingertip tapping a document, saying: "Time is running out." I recalled sneaking into Denvor's house.

I was busy retracing my steps when I heard hurried footsteps advancing. I looked down into the corridor but couldn't make anything out. The footsteps finally spilled out onto the landing. From where I stood, I could see a teenage girl at the end of the corridor. It was Misty-Anne Daniels, Denvor and Tamara's fourteen-year-old daughter. The girl was tall for her age and lean. She had an athletic flair, which showed in the way she stood tiptoed, leaning over the banister, phone in hand.

"I know, mom. Jeez, I told you my homework's done already," she called down to Tamara, then went to her room, grumbling as she slammed the door shut behind her.

At the same time, the outside post lights sprung up again and the gate rattled back, reminding me how I snuck into the house to begin with. I heard voices entering the house, but they soon fell silent. Moments later I heard the crunch of the guard's heavy footfalls crossing the yard below the balcony. The nausea removed its hold of me and completely subsided, but it was replaced by panic.

I was listening so intently to the guard's movements outside that I didn't notice the next set of footsteps coming up the stairs. When I sensed another presence outside the room, I returned to the closet and slowly closed the doors, careful not to make a sound. I drew in another breath, swallowed softly, and became a statue.

An obscure shadow entered the room – and with it returned my intent. I remembered why I was there. I brought up the memory of the night my brother had been shot, how the shadows had parted for but a moment to reveal Denvor in the parking lot, then the rest of the people involved. Without any possibility of restraint, Brenda's face came to me. Anger bled into my confusion. I lifted the weapon and took aim at Denvor's back. This was my moment to claim justice, to fight back for Allan, my mother, Satí, and especially for Brenda. I was prepared to sacrifice my innocence for this moment of justice. I wanted my vengeance so badly. It tasted like poison in my mouth.

Until little Erwin Daniels grumbled, twitched his legs and cooed loudly.

I looked along the barrel of the weapon, over the tip of the silencer, and into Erwin's sleepy eyes. He was staring up at me through the slats in the closet door. The sight of the baby filled me with ice. A cold fist wrapped around my body and began squeezing life out of me. The burst of adrenaline surging through my veins evaporated and clarity washed over me. Then my clarity became my judgement. Whether because I had my gun pointed at a baby's tiny head or whether I had just returned from another one of my spells, I couldn't say. *What on earth did you hope to accomplish?*

At that moment I realized that my presence there was as criminal as the crimes I hoped to avenge. I was not welcome in that place, in that house, at that present moment. It was the grey area where the lives of the innocents and the sins of the diseased converged – and I was in danger of crossing over from one group to the other, even if by accident. *You've gone too far.* I suspect a part of me, the part that operated my fractured mind while I was in the throes of a spell had already crossed the divide and was waiting for the rest of me to arrive. My revenge plans suddenly seemed ill-conceived and pointless. It was as if my drive for revenge had metastasized into something far more severe, much like the cancer pulling my strings, forcing me into a space where I had never intended to go.

Baby Erwin's eyes drew shut and he drifted back to sleep. His arm twitched as he grumbled, then a profound stillness came over him. I leaned forward and rested my perspiring forehead against the closet doors. I closed my eyes in deep thought. I made out the faint rasping sound of the infant's breathing. It reminded me of a fine spring morning, seated in a gynaecologist's waiting room, watching a tiny baby girl drift off to sleep in her mother's chubby arms. Brenda was in the toilet cubicle, sobbing by herself, coming to terms with the reality that she would never have children. It was the type of memory that now made death seem like an inviting prospect.

"Here you are," Tamara said in a firm tone.

I leaned back, lowered my weapon, and shifted deeper into the folds of the clothes.

The big figure beside the bed moved, then Blaine Dumeko stepped out of the shadows.

Tamara's tone and demeanour changed. "Oh, it's you. Where's Denvor?"

"He has business," Dumeko said, looking down at his moccasins.

Tamara's shoulder's sagged and a rueful smile took shape on her soft features.

"Business? You mean the whore in Kraaifontein?" Tamara shook her head in disgust. "What a life I picked for myself."

She uncoupled her bracelet and moved toward a small dresser near the closet. She stared at her reflection while removing her earrings. She placed the jewellery on the dresser, turned around, and approached the cot.

"Why did he send you back here? He usually sends Brian or Vuyo to do his dirty work. He even keeps you for himself."

Dumeko didn't move.

"Vuyo has personal matters. And we suspect Brian has turned. He could be with Collins now."

"Brian?" Tamara said, facing Dumeko. Two fingers rested over her lips. "Not Brian, too. It can't be."

"Last Monday we fed him dirt on a dealer with a load in Belhar. Then Zahier and Plankies show up at the exact location we fed him. How can Collins' crew know about a dealer that doesn't exist?"

"But Brian's mother stays just down the road. Why betray Denvor now?"

"I don't get it, either." Dumeko's voice was deep and

contemplative. He moved towards the windows on the other side of the sliding door. His sigh carried a personal or emotional weight with it. "Maybe he was concerned. What happens to his mother when you all move to Highbury? Or maybe Collins got to him another way. Who knows?"

"Like the police got to Lloyd?"

Dumeko looked at Tamara, his eyes betraying a look of shame.

"Yes, I know what happened to Lloyd."

"It was out of my hands. In this business, loyalties are challenged all the time."

Tamara moved closer to him, her oval face and slanted eyes formed an intoxicating mystery in the shadows.

"And you? How long will you stay loyal to Denvor?"

Dumeko bit his lip in restraint. The frown on his face caused his eyebrows to scrunch down over his small eyes.

"Dammit, Tamara, I don't know anymore. Denvor crossed the line when he killed Shane's brother. There will be consequences after Macky's death. It's about to get dangerous. You should leave."

"I'm not leaving without you," Tamara said. She flung her arms around his big shoulders and leaned her cheek against his left arm to keep her eyes on little Erwin. "And I'm not leaving without our boy."

Dumeko gently put his hand over Tamara's hand and said, "And that will be the death of all of us."

CHAPTER 26

The room erupted. Everyone was screaming at the same time, launching accusations at one another. Spittle hung in the air, coating the atmosphere with tension.

I looked at their angry faces, taut lips and squinted eyes. Everything went into slow motion as a wave of nausea came over me. I suspect it was the angle I was looking at that caused my stomach to churn, but I couldn't wrench my eyes away.

Denvor screamed at Dumeko, Vuyo at Plankies, Dumeko at Shane, Brian at Vuyo, Shane at Denvor, Dillon at Errol, Malique at Dillon, Plankies at Malique, and Errol at Brian. Suddenly they all had skin in the game. Every head had a gun pointed at it – except mine.

I closed my eyes and tried to remember where I was, or how I had gotten there, but everything inside my mind went grey as the screaming intensified. I left the room in a dream. In this dream, I stepped out of my body and walked through a doorway. On the other end of the doorway, I found myself standing on a balcony overlooking the pebbled drive of the Daniels property. The post lights were asleep for the night. There was no sign of

215

dogs or security guards. The night had a blue tinge to it, mystical allure. The air was crisp. Silence roamed. I climbed over the railing and slid down a rain gutter, careful not to make a sound. I scaled the side gate and ran down the road as fast as I could.

Many details fail me when trying to relive the last couple of months. I'm unable to retrace my steps. I don't know how I was able to set in motion something so pure while I was secretly planning something so sinister for those who had wronged me. These two sides of my psyche had not been at war with each other. Instead, they were in perfect synergy, working together in the shadows. When I peered into the dark where my thoughts and their secrets wriggled, visions and dizzy spells were quick to dispel sense. Clarity came and went, while confusion lingered, blowing smoke into my mind. The ever-growing tumour and the accompanying treatment had caused such severe cognitive impairment that I became two different people. These two parts of me had collaborated towards a resolve that would bear the appropriate fruit. I cannot say to what extent the one knew about the dealings of the other.

As the screaming continued in the room, my mind wandered further into the abyss, seeking the closure it had designed for itself. After leaving Denvor's house that night, I guided the little Honda back to Camps Bay. At home, I tended to minor cuts and bruises, then began working my way through Bertie September's list of names and account numbers. It was legible enough because I was accustomed to Bertie's handwriting.

I realized that every name on the page was supposed to be fresh in my memory, but it took me a while to reacquaint myself with them. The page contained the names of all the innocents, those who had been hiding in the chaos, their flickering flames dimmed by the furious glare of the criminals around them. These names had been called out to me while I had been plotting my revenge, reaching through my anger, finding purchase somewhere in the soil of my corroding mind, where Bertie stumbled onto them. They had sprouted there and had become special to me.

Later that night, I paid most of my money to those names, as I had apparently prearranged with Bob Sampson and my banking institutions. I transferred R167 million to twenty-five people in equal portions, the last of which was to a fund in the name of Jayden Makwetu, which was to be facilitated by his mother until he turned twenty-one. The other twenty-four people who received these anonymous payouts were all related or closely linked in some way to the people I had been planning to kill. While I fostered no sympathy towards these cruel men, I had found compassion for those who were pulled along in their wake. They were the remnants of good that spilled out in bits after evil vacated.

Brian White's mother, who still prayed for Brian's salvation every night. I had first heard her do this after joining her church group. She spoke of him as only a loving mother could speak of her only child. From Erwin and Misty-Anne Daniels to Jayden Makwetu. The same with Malique's sister who was facing a series of operations. Or Errol Davids' uncle in Mitchell Plain, who raised him after both his parents had passed away. Astrid Spickerman, Damian Stols, Carmen Moodley – all of them, uninvolved and innocent. I poured my fortune into their struggles, in hope that my sacrifice would rescue or retain their innocence when the evil had been stripped from their lives. If I could buy one life with my pain, it would be sorrow well spent.

The mere thought of saving a life seemed like a worthy prize.

I had kept only a small amount for myself. By bribing pimps and druggies, Bertie convinced both Denvor and Shane that I was muscling in on their territory and that I had a stash house where I hid R100 million in cash or drugs. The information we leaked to Detective Xhosa was enough for the police to raid all their storage facilities and to confiscate all their available funds. As anticipated, they both became desperate. Soon after, Shane and Denvor called an alliance to protect their Northern Suburbs trade. Their henchman had abducted me earlier that morning at my house in Camps Bay.

As I envisioned the large grey sock sliding over my head, my vision cleared again. I slowly returned to the room. My ass felt ragged from having remained seated for such a long time. I was still thirsty. My head was throbbing. I had another treatment booked early that evening, though I imagined that I would probably not make it there alive.

"Bring Tamara here now!" Denvor ordered Vuyo, who had his gun levelled at Plankies on the opposite side of the room. "Fetch her now! Now!"

He screamed so loudly that it drowned all the other voices into submission. In all the months spent studying him, I had never seen Denvor this perplexed or moved to action.

"Move and I'll put your eyes out," Shane called to Vuyo from where he towered over me, not removing his weapon from Denvor.

Denvor, having momentarily forgotten his enemy, turned to face Shane, his one eye twitching in irritation.

"I don't care about your woman troubles. It was you! *You* killed Macky, you piece of shit! And you blamed it on the

Rondebosch clique. Deep down I always knew it was you."

I began laughing before Denvor could respond. It was a fit of hysteria and I couldn't suppress it. The laughter peeled out of me as though it had a mind of its own. My hysterical spells usually ended with me breaking something, but at that moment I just wanted to laugh.

Shane looked at me as though I had interrupted him. Everyone stood on the edge of a precipice, aware that the slightest move would set off a series of gunshots.

"You are all so sick. Poisoned. You can't see a thing in the dark," I said when my laughter dribbled to a low whine. "You probably still think I have money stashed somewhere." That revelation caused me to laugh again.

Shane, the only one without any innocents in his life, shifted his weapon down and held it to my head when he heard about the money. Macky Collins' death had impacted Shane quite a bit, but not enough to make him forget about the possibility of easy money. He was a cold, strange creature.

"The money? Are you shitting me, *bra*?" he whispered. "You have no money? I need that money."

I smiled at him for a long time, counting down the seconds as they stretched out in my mind. His glare was cold and determined, but there hid a glimmer of defeat.

"Because of your menace, I had R167 million to my name," I said.

"Had?" asked Shane in a strained voice. He began tapping the gun's barrel against my head, building himself up. "Where is that money?"

"I gave it all away. I gave it to Astrid Spickerman, Damian Stols, Carmen Moodley, Erwin and Misty-Anne Daniels, Bethany

White, Jayden Makwetu, Hilary and Steffy Bredenkamp, Nosipho Moyana, Hilton Julies…"

"Are those names supposed to mean something to me?"

"… Hilton Julies, Vincent Dumeko, Karim Limba …"

"Shut up!" he screamed so loudly that his afternoon breath fell over my face. "Shut up!"

I scanned the faces in the room and saw I had reached everyone. "Only when you all die," I said, "will their portions pay out. In death, you will give them a second chance at a normal life. At least then you will have some worth."

"I don't know these names," Shane said in a grating voice, his head flicking from Denvor to me. "Where's *my* money? Where's the money!" he kept screaming louder and louder.

I leaned close to Shane, forcing him to make eye contact with me, allowing him to look death in the eyes.

"I tried with all my might to find something pure in your life," I said slowly. "But you are pure evil. You hurt those who enter your sphere without impunity. Even in death, you have no worth. I donated your portion to a schooling initiative in Zambia."

When he heard this, Shane lost himself. He spat at me, swung the barrel at my face and struck me across the cheek so hard that blood spewed into my mouth. The chair I sat in was flung back by the force, which caused me to roll across the floor, from plastic to cement. Blood dribbled over my lips, turning black when it splattered on the dusty surface of the cement.

I pushed myself into a seated position and stared wanly at Shane, ready for the final blow. My head was spinning as the spell worsened. A blinding light came over me. I trembled. I was ready for death.

Shane raised his weapon and put it to my temple. The tip of

his finger drew back across the trigger guard, but it never reached the trigger. A loud compacted blast bounced back from the walls.

A bullet struck Shane high in the chest, ripping through his shirt and ploughing into his flesh. He was pulled off his feet by the impact. He became airborne momentarily, white sneakers dangling comically as he was flung through the air, then crashed to the floor with a muffled rumbling sound. As I turned to look at him, I lost my balance and fell backward. I did nothing to stop the fall. I yielded to the peak of the spell and let go. My head hit the cement. My vision blurred and my ears buzzed.

There was another report, then another seventeen shots in quick succession. *Bam, bam, bam…* Nineteen shots in total. One shy of twenty. The consecutive gunfire had been so loud and so fast that it was jarring to experience, even while lying down.

There followed a long, uncertain silence.

I waited for the spell to subside. It left my body in waves, like the slow withdrawal of a seizure.

The smell of gunpowder settled over me. It stung my nostrils and caused my eyes to water. On the upside, it drew me from my daze far faster than anything else I had tried before.

I sat up, fighting back the urge to throw up. I scanned the room and saw blood on every wall. Not nearly as much as I thought I would see, but enough to realize that weaponry yielded injury. There were confined red splatter marks at obscure angles across the white paint interspersed with gaping holes in the plasterwork.

I pushed myself into a crouched position, then got to my feet. My knees crunched from having been in a seated position for so long. The cut inside my mouth burned furiously. I was still thirsty, and my bladder was ready to burst.

Dillon Moyana groaned softly behind me. I was no doctor, but his face was missing a nose and an upper lip. I was not convinced he would survive the night. A glance confirmed that everyone had been shot at least once, some twice. Here and there, blood had started pooling on the floor, but the cement powder caked it into doughy patches.

I made my way across the room, swiping at the smoke that hung in the air. I was sure I picked up the smell of faeces and urine as I crossed the room. I assumed someone had defaecated themselves when the release of death had taken hold. I wanted to get out of this mess. What I had set out to do had been done. I had no more purpose, so I no longer belonged in that room.

I gripped the cold lever in my shaky hand, shifted upwards until it sprung loose, then pushed the window outward. It was large enough for me to fit through.

"Why?" I heard Denvor's faint voice below me. "Why do all of this just to make a point?"

He had fallen awkwardly near the window, with his head pressed up against the skirting. He looked uncomfortable, though the small hole in his stomach might have contributed to his unease. The blood looked dark. It was thick with a mucous-like viscosity, a stark contrast as it bubbled out of his body and dribbled over his mustard-coloured shirt. His face looked a couple shades whiter than before. His lips had a blueish tinge, and his hair was matted back with sweat.

Based on the way he had fallen and the positioning of his weapon, it was clear he had shot Blaine Dumeko. When I turned to look at Dumeko, I immediately regretted it. His throat had been flayed open, revealing the inner workings of the throat and windpipe in a grotesque manner. I fought back another wave of nausea and turned back to Denvor.

"Why..." He licked his lips with marked difficulty. "Why give it all away to strangers?" His voice was so soft now that I had to lean close to hear him.

"Because I'm already dead," I whispered.

Using the last of his reserves, Denvor raised his weapon at me. The barrel seemed unsure of its direction, swinging this way and that, until Denvor forced his failing eyes to focus. He took short, strained breaths, his chest barely lifting.

I closed my eyes to welcome the bullet. I could taste the blood in my mouth, could smell it in the room, and feel it in my veins. My mind became still. Just as before, there came a final bark of gunfire, but again no surrender of death.

Behind me I heard a grunt. I turned, just in time to see a bloodied Shane stammer forward and topple over Brian White's corpse. When I turned back to Denvor, he had no life left in his eyes and the gun in his hand rested in his lap.

I shimmied out the window as the door flew open. Two armed men stared down at the mess on the floor. I dropped out of sight, disappearing into the shrubbery below the window.

I waited there for a minute or two, then crawled to the hedge, where a wild hibiscus shrub provided ample cover. I made my way towards the edge of the property and slipped away as the sirens pulled into the bottom of the street. The shrill scream of cop cars tore through the suburban silence, blue lights muted in the daylight.

I walked down to the first available bus terminal and left the northern suburbs behind. My reflection in the terminal partitioning convinced me to go to the restroom. There I cleaned the blood off my face. My eye was badly swollen, and my lip and cheek were cut open along the inside of my mouth. I drank some water, gathered myself and caught the bus back into the city.

About an hour later, I was in Camps Bay again. I walked the rest of the way.

When I arrived at the clinic, death welcomed me home once more. I felt the door emit a pleasant sucking sound as it drew shut behind me. There was a new nurse at the reception desk. I could tell she was new because her smile was still sincere.

"I'm here for my treatment," I said.

"Sure, can I please have your name?"

"It's Graybert September," I said. "But you can call me Gray."

ABOUT THE AUTHOR

Besides writing crime novels, James is also a screenwriter, producer, and a wine and travel journalist with a Master's Degree in Creative Writing. Visit his website here.

Follow him on Facebook, Instagram, YouTube, Threads, TikTok, and LinkedIn on this handle: @jamesfouchewrites

He has created a crime drama TV series called Crossing Borders. Watch the proof-of-concept video for free by clicking here.

If you want to connect with James about speaking events or travel and wine reviews, you can reach him on info@jamesfouche.com